AVALON ASSIGNMENT

Emery Grover

The Avalon Assignment

The Assignment Series, Volume 2

E.L. Grover

Published by E.L. Grover, 2024.

THE AVALON ASSIGNMENT

First edition. May 18, 2024.

Copyright © 2024 E.L. Grover.

ISBN: 979-8224896677

Written by E.L. Grover.

All my friends and family who have kept pushing me to do this.

1

Shaikh watched as the nurse finished checking the woman's vitals and handed her a glass of juice with orders to drink it all. She had not been abused, but she was malnourished, the pirates apparently had not understood her nutritional needs. Gamma Squadron had done her a favor in that alone.

The file held little information; three swipes of his finger and he reached the end. In the grand scheme, this woman was insignificant. An average person, working a run-of-the-mill job, on a colony world. Why did she become a part of this group? Let alone, become a terrorist?

His introspection was interrupted as the door opened. There was a scent of high-quality perfume preceding the bland haired women who entered. Her uniform was similar to his, though a different cut, showing the influence from her homeland of France.

"Colonel Shaikh, starting your observations already?"

He greeted the woman with a smile, "Major Roux."

"Did we really travel all the way across U.N. space for this tiny thing?"

Shaikh nodded and handed over the tablet. "So it would seem."

"How did she manage to not get shot?"

He smiled, "You did not read the After-Action Report."

"I find Captain Jubert's reports to be absolutely *riveting*. Why would I fail to read such a work of military art?"

Shaikh laughed, it was true, the commander of Gamma Squadron could make the most mundane assignment take thirty pages and be as dry as any red wine. It was an art that

Shaikh was certain they trained into commanding officers. The report may have been made tedious to discourage reading.

"She surrendered. Even shot some of her allies beforehand, not that it did anything more than save Gamma the trouble of killing them."

Roux nodded, "Poor girl had probably not even pulled a trigger until she made that choice. She acted to protect her unborn, that was likely the source of her strength at that moment. Now, she has to live with it."

"Rather insightful," Shaikh said.

"Have you spoken to her yet?" Roux asked.

"No, I was waiting for the medical staff to be finished."

"Looks like they are. Let's begin, shall we?"

Shaikh nodded, "I think you should open the conversation."

Shaikh exited the room, giving a nod to the nurse in the hall. She tensed, eyeing him and Roux with soldier-like intensity. He gave a reassuring smile and held his hands about waist high, palms towards her. The nurse stepped aside, allowing them into the room.

"Hello. Leanna, is it? My name is Marie Roux. How are you feeling now that you've gotten some food?"

Leanna looked wide-eyed as they entered, Shaikh noticed she relaxed a bit at the question. After a moment of eyeing the glass on the table, she nodded. "I feel like I'm gonna puke again."

"How far along?" Roux asked with a smile, taking a seat at the table's edge.

"Six months."

"Oh, a wonderful time. You can feel all the unpleasant kicks and turns. It also seems to be a good time for the baby to use your bladder to sleep on."

Shaikh was content to watch the exchange, as it gave him the opportunity to study Leanna. She was lean and pale, but clean. The way she looked between him, and Roux gave him the impression she wasn't going to be hiding anything intentionally. In his experience, this look indicated fear over taking loyalty or reasoning.

"What will happen to me now?"

Shaikh kept his voice pleasant and conversational, "We will speak for a time, then let you rest if needed. Depending on how well our talk goes, you may only have to endure our company once or twice. After that, we will hold you until a local magistrate determines if you are to be charged with any crimes."

"I did nothing wrong!"

Roux reached out and patted the woman's hand on the table, "We know. We must do it though, dear. We must take every step to ensure we follow the law, Oui?"

He could see Leanna's hand tremble under Roux's hand. He knew Roux would keep her touch gentle and pat the girl's hand as she looked at her. Roux would then use that as a building block for more connections.

"If we don't, we'll be seen as violating Tronis' authority," Roux explained. "We don't want that. We only wish what is best for all involved."

"I only went because my boyfriend did," Leanna said. "He said he could get us the money we needed for our own place, but he didn't want to leave me behind."

Roux nodded, "Noble of him."

"We were told that everyone had to contribute. At first, I was confused," Leanna said, "but after I thought about it, I didn't mind contributing."

"Why did you not mind?" Shaikh asked.

Leanna shrugged, "I wanted to feel helpful, and need to keep active. Then, I noticed there was no standard company logo, no orientation classes, so I thought it was a private company, or independents."

"Not a poor thought process," Roux said.

"They had us all doing group workouts, taking turns doing chores, cooking and that sort of thing." Leanna explained, "I couldn't do certain things, and nobody seemed bothered. They just laughed and patted me on the back; then the guns showed up."

Shaikh made some notes in his tablet, wondering just how effective the local tracking satellites were. Solar systems could be treacherous places, with comets, and drifting asteroids. They would need a century to catalog everything and verify the path of every object.

Leanna was crying as she spoke, "I tried to get him to take me home, to explain to him that this was something bad, these people were going to do something terrible to someone else. I didn't want to be part of it, and I didn't want him to be."

Roux nodded, "We always want to see the best in our partners, even if they cannot see it themselves, eh? He was a good man?"

Leanna nodded, wiping away a tear, "Yes. He worked double shifts at the port, he never came home later than the time it took to get home, while other dock hands would go to the bar or go other places and find well. It's difficult for us to..."

Roux held up a hand and smiled, "Ah, young love. I would have been quite happy with such a man; mine had a habit of drinking and fighting. Also, visiting my sister before he would come home."

Leanna made a face, "How'd you settle that?"

"With a kick to his groin and a slap to my sister's face," Roux said, grinning.

Leanna laughed, while Shaikh noted she was no longer trembling and she remained steady while pouring more juice. He absently went over the report again, he wasn't thrilled with the potential information. He was positive that they had uncovered a much deeper plot, though he still needed it corroborated.

"Where did the weapons come from?" Shaikh asked.

Leanna looked back at him and swallowed hard as he watched her expression and body language. She was uneasy, but she was going to tell him the truth. He knew the answer was bad with the return of fear in her voice.

"They were a mixed group. Two Aldrit, the green kind that look like Earth's old stories of aliens, they offered over the crates with no haggling, so I think they were already paid for. They had guards as well," she said.

"They had bodyguards? Who?"

"S-Shezlan."

Shaikh could feel a shift in Roux's demeanor, as well as the glare she was giving him. He resisted the urge to smile and tell her she should have read the report; self-preservation overrode his desire for a well-deserved taunt. He also knew if they started to bicker, Leanna would withdraw, and there were more questions to ask.

"Leanna dear," Roux started, "did you observe any emblems on their uniforms or the ship that ferried them?"

She nodded, "Yes. A trio of stars, with three claws, one below the next. On the other side of the stars was a single angel wing."

Shaikh nodded, "That was on the uniforms?"

"Yes,"

"What about the ship, dear?" Roux asked quietly.

"It had a large star with some squiggly looking lines making a box around it."

Shaikh motioned to the door as he stood, offering an inclination of his head to Leanna. He noticed Roux patted Leanna on her hand and was smiling warmly. He figured she would retaliate by making him wait in the hall.

"You did great child," Roux said. "How old are you?"

"Seventeen."

Roux smiled again and nodded. "Alright dear, we are going to make some calls and discuss some things. I'll have the nurse take you to the observation unit so you can lie down and rest."

"Will you be back?"

"Maybe. I know I will have to ask a few more questions, but I think they can wait until you have slept."

Once Roux joined him in the hall, he left simple instructions to have Leanna taken somewhere to rest, then led the way to his secure office on the station. The office was for visiting officials and thus had a large window to see the colony below.

Roux strode past him into the room, pacing in front of the window. Shaikh briefly imagined her as an angry tiger and reminded himself to handle her with care. They had a long history, but he knew her temper well. The door clicking into place was the perfect catalyst.

"Zut!" Roux growled, "Putain de Shezlan!"

Shaikh laughed, "Do you always go to your native language to curse?"

"Oui! It is more colorful and accurate."

He nodded and sat down, looking at his tablet as it beeped, "Well, it just got worse."

Roux spun again, "How?"

"The journalist with Gamma Squadron? He sent his editor a copy of his report and video."

"Merde!" Roux tossed her hands up.

"Look at this," he said, turning the tablet around.

Roux looked, and her eyes widened. The screen displayed the emblem Leanna had described; an angel wing joined to three claws by a trio of stars. The symbol of the Prides of Thyla's special operations unit, on a uniform being worn by a human.

"Mon Dieu," she whispered, "are they trying to start another war?"

"Maybe. I think first, they are going to destabilize the colonies."

2

Eversley crawled the last few meters to the fence, peering through the dark and grass, around the rocks to watch for the foot patrol. He felt Granberg tap his foot, signaling he was moving up to his side. He glanced for a second, then back to watching for the patrol.

"Overwatch for two-two, I have you at the fence line. The patrol is coming around the far corner, still on pace; twelve seconds," came Andrews' voice.

Eversley keyed the radio, "Copy."

He motioned to Granberg, and both made the careful movement to come to a squatting position. Eversley pulled out his combat knife and made ready, silently counting, though he knew Andrews would call it out. A steady breath and then he saw his target come into view.

"They're in position," Andrews said into his ear.

There was no signal, no verbal call to action between them. He and Granberg simply launched their attack in unison. Eversley came up and felt the moment of resistance as his blade drove into his target's neck, just under the jaw. They fell limp as he wrapped an arm around the body and pulled them into the weeds.

He laid them down, looked at Granberg and blinked. The man was laying his target down, one of his hand-held axes embedded in their face. He shrugged back and pulled his second as he watched for any stray targets.

"Two-two for two-one, we are clear; going to cut in now," Eversley said over the encrypted radio.

"Two-one good copy, we are likewise; making entry," came Holte's reply.

Eversley motioned and Granberg started the rest of the way to the fence with his laser cutter. It would take only a few seconds to have a hole large enough for them to pass through. While waiting, he unslung his rifle and took up overwatch.

A moment later, he felt the tap from Granberg, then moved through the hole in the fence. They moved to a nearby corner of a building and looked inside the camp. There was no movement; it was late, so they figured most would be in bed. The leadership might still be meeting, hopefully in person with someone who had been providing them aid.

"Two-two for Two-one, we are inside."

"Good copy, so are we. Move to target building, you should be able to see it from there."

Eversley peered around the corner, "Yep, I see it. Two guards out back."

The two men were standing near the door, not against the building. Eversley could smell the cigarette one was smoking through his suit's environmental sensors. He could block it, but there was no need in this case, besides, using all his senses helped.

"We've got two out front as well. Lights are on too," Holte said.

Andrews' voice came over the line, "Overwatch here. Hungry eyes is showing five people inside. Thermal has them all sitting in the central room, each one is taking turns at the front. Looks like a briefing if I had to guess."

"Good," came Holte's voice, "let's hope we can catch their benefactor in there. Move up, clear the sentries, and prepare for entry."

Eversley nodded and tapped Granberg on the shoulder. The man came around to his right side, bringing up his rifle and similarly peering around the corner. With their helmets enclosed they could speak, but noise discipline kept them silent and using sign language out of habit. He made a count with his free hand, keeping his other ready to squeeze his trigger.

He closed his fist and moved around the corner, with Granberg at his side. They moved silently towards the door and the guards, who were busy chatting and exchanging the cigarette. He and Granberg got to three meters before one of them looked their way.

Too late. Eversley thought to himself as he squeezed off a controlled burst of fire. They used a modified coil gun, set to subsonic speeds. The clatter hardly registered in his ears and was unlikely to draw attention, still, he winced at the sound. The model was perfectly designed for this sort of operation but had almost no ability to penetrate body armor, leaving him to feel vulnerable.

Granberg had fired as well, taking his down in the same instant. They closed to the door, and Eversley briefly whispered a prayer of thanks. The two had fallen away from the building and not struck it. Once he and Granberg were in position, he whispered into his com,

"Two-two at the door."

"Copy. Two-one as well. Prep for breach."

Eversley nodded and carefully placed an access computer on the door's control. It would take a few seconds, then be ready for a dual entry. He just had to let it do its job, and that was annoying to him. He had argued for Silverling to prepare them some breaching charges, but Keith shot that down. He wanted the primary targets secured before the place turned into a war zone.

"Overwatch to all, hold, hold, hold!"

Eversley flinched and looked at Granberg who was already looking outward for trouble. His mind ran down the list of possible problems. The meeting could be ending, and they'd be walking right out into the team, there was a patrol, or someone suddenly decided to walk out of a building.

"We've got an issue, looks like someone inside suspects. One just popped up and looks like they pulled a sidearm."

Eversley heard Holte's teeth grind through the com before she spoke, "Go loud, breach, breach, breach!"

He wasted no time, overriding the device safety, causing it to blow the door open. A small shower of sparks flew about as he and Granberg moved through. Weapons up, they activated the speakers on their suits; loud sonic pulses proceeding them, causing confusion in the room ahead.

He added to it by tossing a flashbang around the corner, through the next doorway, calling it out to his team just before releasing. The thud he felt was marginal, and he briefly recalled what it felt like without the suit's defenses.

He moved in fast, scanning for anyone still up; one man raised a weapon as someone went out a side door. Eversley's movements resulted from years of training. A brief burst of rounds struck the man center-mass, dropping him to the floor.

"Runner, runner, runner!" He called as he swept for any other threats.

Holte and Qureshi were on top of two before they could regain their senses. Granberg grabbed one who was about halfway to their feet, using one arm he lifted them and then drove them to the floor. Eversley heard a feminine yelp as Granberg pinned his target to the floor and was zip tying her hands.

"This is Overwatch. I've got 'em, moving east and fast! Looks like the whole place is waking up!"

Eversley moved to follow the runner, seeing a window they had apparently dove out of. They were just moving past a building. He moved to the frame, but Holte's voice stopped him.

"Let 'em go! That's Keith's job, let's prep for evac!"

Eversley nodded and after one last glance out the window, moved to cover the door he and Granberg had come through. He saw people starting to stream out of the various buildings, some half-dressed, some in fatigues, a couple perhaps wearing armor.

"Here comes trouble!" He called as he started to fire at the ones who moved towards their position.

In the same instant, several explosions rocked the ground. Buildings vanished in fireballs all around them, and the rumbling sound of the lander shook the area. He smiled and moved back into the room with the others.

"Looks like our ride is here," he said.

Holte nodded to him and motioned him to lead them out, "Thump should be right outside in just a second."

"That's the part that scares me," he replied as he moved past to the hallway and looked outside.

As he expected, the lander was pivoting so it could come down just in front of their position. Streaks of laser fire erupted from the various gun ports on the craft. Missiles, hard mounted to the side, roared off, a moment later the explosions were heard.

Once the lander was down, the side door slid open and Eversley called out to the rest of the team to move. He watched for anyone trying to fire their direction amid the chaos. There were several, but the lander's point defense seemed to make quick work of the people in sight.

"Last one," said Granberg as he patted his shoulder.

Eversley backed up and climbed into the lander. He felt the craft lurch under his feet, the G-force of the acceleration almost taking him to the floor; he was thankful for the overhead handles at that moment. He looked and saw Qureshi, Holte, and Granberg all present, as well as, their three guests, and an armload of tablets.

"Hey folks," he said as he squatted down to look at one captive, "comfy?"

"Fuck off Earther," one man said as he spat.

Eversley just smiled, "Well that's not very nice."

"Hey," came Holte's voice, "knock it off."

Eversley nodded and keyed his mic, "Two-two for One-one."

Keith's voice came back on the line, "Go for One-one."

"You get that squirter?"

There was laughter on the line, "You mean the one you let get away?"

"Fuck too! I had their ass till Holte called me off!"

Eversley grinned and looked over to the petty officer first class, she was giving him a dirty look and flipping him off. He just laughed, as he settled against the bulkhead to ride out the flight to base. He adjusted his helmet and noticed he had a closed call from Keith.

"What's up Chief?"

"Our squirter suicided. Clacked off a bomb large enough to have leveled that building."

Eversley shook his head, "Damn. Get an ID?"

"Nope, nothing official anyway."

"What's your gut say?"

"Shezlan."

Eversley let out a long breath, that was not good. He trusted Keith, the man had a knack for knowing what was what on the field, if he thought he saw something, he probably did. That also meant there was an alien presence, and Shezlan at that.

"So, what now brother?"

"We tell Jubert and make our reports. We also keep our heads on a swivel out in the field, this changes the game."

Eversley nodded to himself, "Copy that."

He settled in and stared across the way as the line closed. The war was long over, but it felt like someone wanted to get back into it. All that destruction on Earth, lives lost, colonies burnt to cinders, and some idiot humans with delusions of who knew what wanted the Shezlan's help to do something that made Earth weaker.

He looked over at the three people they had sitting against the bulkhead in restraints. Qureshi and Granberg were watching them. Eversley smiled to himself, they were huddled close to each other, the ones on the ends each trying to keep away from the operator staring at them. While most smart people were afraid of Granberg, he knew no one understood the danger Qureshi posed. She took the betrayal of humanity personally.

Not that anyone else didn't, he reminded himself, but she just had this extra spice about it. When they had debriefed after the pirate station, she was livid about the intel discoveries. He still didn't understand all the words she used, he wasn't fluent in Arabic, but they certainly didn't sound very friendly. Keith had pulled her aside after and they had a long chat. He could only imagine what it was about; Keith had pulled him aside once and reminded him how he was to conduct himself.

Eversley briefly allowed himself a smile at the thought. Keith and Jubert just had a way, a code of conduct that was above the regulations. They pushed the team hard to adhere to it. Everyone had learned a lesson or two at the hands of their leadership.

It's also why we're the best. he thought to himself.

The rest of the trip was smooth, he didn't even notice the landing. He figured Thump had finally figured out how to land, but the shouting from the front told him that Jaw Jack had likely taken the call on the landing and was rubbing it in her face.

Eversley stood up and helped the others make their guests ready to disembark. It took little to get them up, the weight of the situation having settled in on the flight back, they hadn't said a thing and just stood. The defiance was there, but not the spirit.

He and Granberg were on either side of the trio with Qureshi leading down the ramp. Eversley glanced back and saw Holte had a satchel with the tablets slung over her shoulder as she moved in step behind them. The soldiers at the base had come out and were in a small circle around the lander, watching the escort.

"We will take it from here Gamma Squadron," came an unfamiliar voice with an accent he couldn't place.

Eversley looked at Holte and then at the person speaking. Their uniform was prim and proper, orderly, and devoid of any sort of insignia. That told him more than anything else; United Nations Intelligence Services.

3

Keith flipped through the tabs on his tablet while sitting at the table seeing the same words, in different reports, from his team. None of the information deviated, all the same sterile after-action reports. He could quote the entire report by now.

He glanced up at Commander Jubert, the old man was equally bored it seemed, having given up on his tablet, he was looking out the observation window. Keith still thought he looked carved out of stone, just standing there looking, his calm demeanor and shallow breathing giving very little away.

"Did you die on me over there?"

Jubert looked back and smirked, "Not yet, just preparing to deal with the spooks."

"This Colonel, Shieak? Seak? Ceek?"

"It's Shaikh," came a voice from the doorway.

Keith stood as the man entered, studying him. He was lean built, with a very military cut, precisely aligned buttons, and lack of the sun's touch on his caramel skin. He was under the impression the man hadn't been on a planet in about a year.

"Sorry Colonel."

The man waved it off as he took a seat, "I've found those from outside my corner of Earth tend to mispronounce many names."

Keith nodded and once Jubert took his seat, he joined them, "Judging by the accent, I'm going to guess India?"

"Fair guess, chief petty officer."

Commander Jubert cleared his throat, "I'm sure the Colonel has a reason for us to be here, besides guessing his hometown."

"I do. That said, I do try to keep people comfortable. It makes conversation easier."

Keith watched Jubert's response, the raised eyebrow and leaning forward, it was a way to gauge his own responses in the conversation. They hadn't been told why the Intelligence Agency wanted to speak with them. Recent events likely meant it had to do with their missions around Tronis.

The Colonel nodded, "True. I must inform you that what we are about to discuss is classified and only for those with a need-to-know. Moving forward, Gamma Squadron will be operating under my task force."

Keith nodded, that was hardly news. He noticed Jubert did as well and motioned the colonel to continue. People with top level clearance made up the special operations teams anyway, so it wasn't likely that the spook had much more access.

"To start off, we interviewed the young woman you captured during your recent hostage rescue mission. Excellent work, by the way."

He felt Jubert's eyes on him for a moment, and Keith could only shrug, "We appreciate that. I take it the talk was productive?"

"Yes, that gave you the information for your most recent mission. She gave us some names of people her boyfriend talked about that weren't at the station you hit. From there, well, the pieces fell in nicely and we could track down their meeting places."

Keith understood the reasoning behind it, but he felt disappointed that his team wasn't asked to run the surveillance operation. Still, the fact he let them run the take down was a good sign. It likely meant the team would stay involved, and this wasn't a kiss off.

"May I ask who planned the mission?"

Jubert beat him to the answer, which caused a slight smile, "As is typical, our operators on the ground do the planning. In this instance, Petty Officer First Class Holte was the primary. Once she designed the game plan, she passed it to Keith, who approved and gave it to me."

The colonel nodded, "I see. A large amount of autonomy and self-reliance breeds creativity. The operation went well, even if it was a touch, simplistic."

"Simple plans have less to go wrong," Keith said.

"True. So, while I do appreciate that sort of initiative and training, moving forward I would prefer mission planning remained in both of your hands; in whatever manner you typically conduct such."

"Why is that?" Jubert asked.

"Put simply," Shaikh said, "I would rather Gamma be operating at full and proper efficiency."

Keith drummed his fingers on the table as he watched Jubert simply lean back in his seat. It wasn't uncommon to be tasked with an intel officer, and they had ways they wanted to go about things, but something about the colonel's demeanor said it wasn't just about efficiency.

If the acceptance surprised the colonel, Keith couldn't read it. The man looked between them and went back to his tablet a moment. An instant later, a hologram appeared in the middle of the table, a rendering of the photos recovered from their hostage rescue. It was of the patch on some uniforms the pirates had been wearing.

"I'm sure you do not need the explanation, but, indulge me. This patch belongs to a special operations group from the Prides of Thyla," Shaikh said, "specifically one they refer to as a deep reconnaissance and exploitation pack."

"Basically, the Shezlan equivalent to the old Green Berets," Keith said.

Shaikh nodded, "Very much. Go behind enemy lines, train locals, and become force multipliers."

"So, the Prides are using covert operations instead of open war this time," said Jubert.

"To start with yes, that is how it seems."

Keith sat in silence as he listened to them discuss the implications. Covert operations weren't all that strange a game plan, and certainly a good opening act, the only concern he had was this seemed to be on the wrong front. They were bypassing a lot of territory to operate on the far side of United Nations' space. The larger worry was, had they operated closer already?

There had been no acts of piracy, nor had there been any insurrection amid the colonies closest to the border of Shezlan territory. The burning and bombardment during the war likely resulted in no purchase in those areas. There was also the case they just didn't want to risk it and instead attacked the weakest unity.

Keith let his mind wander down the paths of tactics. Tronis, amid many of the colonies not attacked, had made no secret about issues with Earth's government. They made for ripe grounds for a task force that specialized in this sort of warfare. Shezlan were historically very cautious of humans though, so what drove them to decide it was worth, well whatever the issue was with humanity?

"Chief?"

Jubert's voice broke his concentration, causing him to look up. He glanced between both men and then to the holo, it was showing the local system and nearby hyper jump points. He saw several red pinpoints, likely locations of interest his team would be checking out or raiding for intel.

"Sorry, brainstorming till needed."

"I see, well, at this point I would appreciate your input. The commander has made it clear you are quite the field commander."

Keith looked over at Jubert and smirked a moment before looking back over, "So what do you need?"

"I have several intel targets in mind, and I would like you to review them. Also, there is the need to sift through the intelligence you gathered late last night."

"Nothing my team can't do, sir. We've had to read on site intel and make game plans from what we've gathered."

The colonel nodded, "I find that acceptable. I will be reviewing items as well so that your people are not carrying the bulk."

"Also," Jubert chimed in, "the Australia is being redeployed, which means we no longer have that bit of support."

Keith felt a pit in his stomach.

"So, play nice with the local militia weekend warriors," Jubert said.

"Aye, sir."

The colonel looked between them both, "Something I should be aware of?"

"Nothing serious, I just sort of stomped on the Tronis Director's toes about them sending troops on the hostage rescue. I don't like putting my team's lives in the hands of,"

"Amatures?"

Keith nodded, "Yes sir."

"I can understand that, even appreciate it, however Gamma is not that large of a force. We can't hit all these potential locations at once with just your team. I don't have time to bring more operators out."

Keith nodded, "I understand that hindrance, my only issue is mixing teams. If you want to deploy them on a target or two, I'm fine with that, but mixing with my team is a disaster waiting to happen."

"If you and your team can build solid plans, and they demonstrate the skill needed, I see no reason to mix them with your team. Although I may wish for some to be in place for overwatch and as advisors."

Commander Jubert nodded, "I think that is a workable trade off. I'd like to have the Chief build one squad specifically to keep for priority targets. A secondary squad as a quick reaction force and divvy a third as the oversight."

Keith agreed, "The numbers will work out well. Give us a chance to sort through the equipment and give it all some tune up."

"You don't keep your equipment maintained?" Asked Shaikh.

"We do, but we do have to adapt it to the environment. Tronis is different from Earth in terms of air density, gravity, and temperature ranges. All this plays into the equipment, especially coil guns." Keith said.

"I see. Moving on, do you have particular people in mind to use as observers with the militia? Or do you plan to ask for volunteers?"

"I've got a couple I will ask," Jubert said, "as well as a couple that I plan to... encourage."

"You mean a couple to be voluntold?" Keith asked.

Jubert shrugged, "Some just need the encouragement."

Keith laughed, that was Jubert's way. Pick someone who had potential, and if they didn't see it, make them see it. He had been through the same ordeal when Jubert first recruited him to Gamma. He remembered it fondly in the moment, even used the same tricks on Holte and Eversley.

"I see. I suspect you will seek mission success, so those you send will be the best candidate you have available," Shaikh said.

Keith and Jubert both nodded, they didn't want things to fail. Keith looked at the situation overall and started pondering who he'd like to be in those positions. There were a few candidates on the team he figured could use the experience.

"I think the only problems we will have is, the team members being annoyed they aren't on one of the two standby teams," Jubert said.

Keith nodded, "I'm inclined to agree. They'll do the job as oversight, but they'll make a point of it being a temporary ordeal."

"I would hope it does not become a permanent assignment. My goal is to have these groups swept up in the next few months."

Keith nodded, "Sounds reasonable."

"What if we find a Shezlan in the mix?" Asked Jubert.

Shaikh nodded, "Ah yes, the crux of this all. Any such individual who is discovered is to be taken into custody. At least, I want it attempted. Shezlan seem to have a very strong stigma against such a thing."

Keith blinked, "Warrior's code, maybe?"

Shaikh shook his head, "I think not. There are no cultural references that we have to detail they operate under such a code. They have rules of engagement, after a fashion, and what has been provided in small interactions officially has them being very much possessed of a reverence for their lives."

"So how does that play into suicide? I seem to recall many attacks, that were kamikaze attacks, on Earth's surface," Keith commented.

Shaikh shrugged, "So much more the reason to bring one in alive and question them."

4

John watched the team do their meticulous work in silence, his camera panning over the workspace. They had set tables up to strip weapons down, others to sort packs of equipment or ammunition. They made it all look like an ant colony; busy worker ants focused on their tasks. There was music, more of the heavy drum pounding tribal-yelling the team seemed to like so much. He wasn't sure what language it was, but it sounded like something guttural and visceral.

"Well, not going to learn anything from here," he told himself.

A quick glance showed him who was doing what, and he settled with trying Eversley's table; he had been willing to talk to him more since the incident on the pirate base. It was clearly time to capitalize on that good grace and build. As he moved over toward the table a few he passed looked up, but only enough to see who moved past them.

When he got to the table, Eversley had a large coil gun taken apart. The magnetic coils were laid out in a line, the power cable was stretched out, and Eversley was using a small tool to take yet another coil from the rifle's housing. John waited until the delicate work was done before speaking.

"Can I ask some questions about all this?"

Eversley looked up and nodded, "Sure, I'm pretty sure nothing here is classified."

John smirked, "Well good. So, what are you doing?"

"Recalibrating this coil gun. See here," he pointed with his small tool, "there are all these tiny adjustment points? They regulate the energy going into the coil, thereby, how much pull it has."

John nodded as he watched the work being done, "So why does this have to be done?"

"Mostly upkeep. I want the equipment in the best possible state. There is also the fact I've got to make it function here on Tronis."

"You have to make it work differently here?"

Eversley nodded and made a tiny adjustment to the piece in his hand. He then connected a clip to it, which was linked to a tablet, started to open a menu and was adjusting some sliders under various headers.

"Yep, the magnetic field each coil produces needs to be made to work with the local gravity field."

"So for every planet, moon or asteroid you're on you have to adjust these?"

Eversley nodded, "Pain in the ass, isn't it?"

"Sounds it. Is the effect so bad?"

"Can be. For example, on Tronis, this weapon system has a rise of about one inch over a hundred yards when calibrated for Earth."

"Is that a lot?"

Eversley chuckled, "You don't do a lot of shooting do you Newsie?"

John felt a smile on his face, "Not really."

"Alright, so that's the difference between aiming here," he felt a solid tap to his chest that took the wind out of his lungs for a second, "and here," and there was a follow up thump in the top of his chest.

After a quick intake of air, John managed to find his voice, "So the heart and the chest, aren't I still dead?"

Eversley shrugged, "Depends on the armor you are wearing and how solid a hit I get. For spray and pray, it's fine, for the type of shooting we do, it's unacceptable."

John nodded, he knew the team took pride in their skill, clearly he hadn't given enough credit to how much they did for it. He looked around at the other work going on and figured it was much the same. When he looked back, Eversley was placing the coil he was working on back into its housing.

"That makes sense for worlds, what about star bases or on ships?"

Eversley shrugged at him, "That gets tricky, we can approximate and do a quick setting on the side of the system here," he pointed to a screen on the top of the weapon, "I can make some small adjustments, so long as it's not too far out from the baseline the coils are at."

"How do you get a reading for the gravity on a station?"

Eversley motioned to his face, "Our visors on the combat suit."

John nodded, once he thought about it, things made more sense. "I suppose stations are probably closer to their home planet's gravity setting anyway, aren't they?"

Eversley nodded, "Yep, that helps too."

"Thanks, I think I'll go pester the others for some insights."

He received a fist bump, and as he turned to look for his next conversation, he felt the smile on his face grow again. Things were going much better with the team and he wasn't being run off. He spotted Stewart and moved that direction.

"Hey Newsie, what's up?"

John stepped around the table, taking in the site, all the gauze, tapes, and odd-looking tools. The collection looked impressive, just strange to him. He was sure he saw a couple of auto tourniquets as well.

"Well, going around getting B-reel footage and asking questions about how things are done. So, what are you working on?"

Stewart nodded. "Only the good things my man. Also, something for you to have, by the way."

"Me?" John asked, a bit surprised.

"Yes you. One of these specifically," he said, motioning to a mid-sized bag on the table. "You'll be carrying extra trauma tools, but everyone in the field carries a personal use bag."

John blinked, "I hadn't thought of that."

Stewart laughed, "Yeah, no one does till they need it. Order of safety is self-care before buddy care. You do what you can, and if you need help, then you call it in."

"Why is that?"

"Honestly, battlefield dynamics. If you are in a firefight, a wounded individual takes two or more out of the fight."

John started to understand, "Ah, so you try to treat the wound alone, keep the others in the fight until things calm down."

"Yep. Everyone in the field carries one of these bags full of what they need to start. You get one too."

John nodded, "I'm not first aid trained, so how's that going to work?"

"You get educated, that's how," Stewart said, the jovial tone in his voice dipped slightly.

"Guess I know what's next on my list."

Stewart nodded. "Good."

Before he could ask the next question, the door of the room opened, and Commander Jubert strode in. "Huddle up!"

John watched everyone instantly drop what they were doing and move towards the commander. He set his camera drone to follow and moved with the rest of them. Not standing with the team, but to the side so he could watch and record.

"New orders came in. We are working with UN Intelligence Services, chasing down more of these suspected cells," he started out.

John panned the group as they finished settling in, some on the floor sitting, others on a knee, and a small set standing. Their faces were neutral masks, as near as he could tell, taking in what was being said and trusting the Commander.

"Operationally nothing major changes. We are here to finish what we started and find these groups that are being supplied and funded by extraterrestrial governments," Jubert said.

John noticed he let that sink in, and the team exchanged looks. In that moment, he caught some expressions of surprise, some of anger, and some appeared to be thinking about some detail or another. It was in these moments he wished he was a telepath, not that any human had ever been officially documented as one.

"We will be sorting out in three elements moving forward. A single strike team, a quick reaction force," Jubert studied them before finishing, "and an overwatch and observation team."

Silverling raised her hand first, "Why are we dedicating an entire team to overwatch, and what do you mean by observation?"

"One team will be operating with the Tronis military, serving as their overwatch and providing in field oversight to their operations. There are too many targets for us to hit at once, so they will be helping."

Everyone in the room made a face, various annoyed expressions, John even felt his own annoyance rising. He shoved it back down and went back to documenting and studying, though there were no voices of dissent he noticed.

Eversley raised a hand, "That the UNIS's idea?"

Jubert shook his head, "No, the Chief and I made this call."

Everyone muttered amid themselves for a moment, there was anger in some tones, and surprise in others. John couldn't make it all out from where he was, but he could guess. Gamma was a tight group, a family, and avoided outside influence, or outsiders in general; he'd experienced that firsthand.

"I get it, you don't like it. Tough," Jubert said firmly.

The room went silent, everyone's eyes went back to the commander. John liked how the man could reign them in, but it even made his thoughts stop a moment. He waited for Jubert's next words before he remembered to breathe. He was suddenly glad he was one of the good guys.

"Holte, you'll be running the QRF. I'll give you Bekele, George, Turgenev, Andrews and Eversley."

John watched the team nod as they got their assignments, he had been around enough to understand the lingo and the breakdown. George, he knew, was a combat medic like Stewart, he hadn't spoken to him much, but he could pick him out of a crowd. Turgenev was nice enough, he was going to be their fire support, John knew that instantly. He loved his large coil gun.

"Granberg, Qureshi, Stewart, Silverling, and Harrison, you are with Keith on the strike team."

There was a brief cascade of laughter as those who remained knew what they were in for. Jubert didn't mince words, pointing them out and telling them what unit they'd be overseeing. John chuckled at the jeering and poking that occurred. Then, he noticed a small smile on Jubert's face; it was gone as soon as he got his camera up.

"Alright, get back to work. I want all gear ready for inspection by thirteen hundred. Newsie, come with me," Jubert said.

John jumped. It had been some time since he and Jubert spoke. He set his drone back to roaming and followed Jubert out the door. His mind was racing as to what this could be about, briefly wondering if the news report he had sent back caused the man some issues. The thought made him sick, causing Gamma trouble was not what he wanted.

Out in the hall, he saw a man dressed in a nondescript-looking uniform. He could see no rank, only a patch he was unfamiliar with. There was a calm about the man, and he had the sense he had seen him before this.

"Newsie, this is Colonel Shaikh UNIS," Jubert said.

Jon nodded, "Colonel, good to meet you sir. What's this about?"

"Straight to the point, I like that," Shaikh said.

The line seemed contrived and rehearsed to John. There was a pit forming in his stomach, he wasn't sure exactly why but, he wanted to be anywhere but near this guy. That in itself told him all he needed to know, this man was a type of trouble John didn't want.

"I see no sense in beating around the bush, you have work, I'm sure, and I have a story to work on," John said.

Shaikh nodded, "I agree. In short, Mister Aerovant, I am here to tell you that your pass to film Gamma Squadron is being suspended."

"Excuse me?"

"I don't think you need any explanation, it is rather simple," Shaikh said.

John blinked, "You don't have the authority to suspend that."

"Don't I? I am responsible for the safety and integrity of all UNIS operations, and Gamma Squadron is currently operating under UNIS, so I get final say."

"At most you can limit my access, not deny it. The Media and Press Act says as much."

"True, that said your filming and presence is restricted to base."

John took in a deep breath, he knew it would happen eventually. "Then you can apply to have my pass amended, from the office that issued it. That would take time, time I would promptly use to make it clear UNIS wanted the press limited."

Shaikh looked at him, "Your father must have told you how limited your power is in this case, that action would immediately render your pass mute, and make your father quite the figure in the closed circles."

"Maybe, but not before he made your boss feel the pain of it. No matter how things fall, you'll still have to answer for whatever trouble your boss must contend with from an Admiral."

"Your footage is still to be surrendered after any mission into the field. I will be the one reviewing it."

"That's fair. I'll be expecting all the documentation that goes with it."

Shaikh nodded, and turned to walk off, "Worry not, all explanations will be legal and in full."

John waited until the man was out of the hall and the building before letting out his held breath. Jubert patted him on the shoulder, and when he looked over, it surprised him to see the man smiling.

"Ballsy, not the best choice, but ballsy," Jubert said.

5

Director Hawthorn watched as the pilot keyed the radio to contact the star base looming in the near distance. He looked over the incomplete sections and smiled, the colony's first off world structure was about to be finished. There was a sense of pride building inside as he saw it in person. It helped that he was transporting the Colony Director and the Commerce Minister for their official tour.

"Avalon station, this is shuttle TC-one, making an approach to landing bay two."

The return caller was immediate and proper, "This is Avalon station, you are cleared to land in bay two. The doors are open, be welcome."

Hawthorn was surprised at the smoothness of the landing, there was no actual feeling of change in gravity, and no clunky shifting of the ship's orientation to the station. When touring orbital satellites, he had been jostled around due to improper calibration of the gravity well. Ships would shake, twist, and on one occasion creak loudly as the fields would clash with one another.

Upon exiting the shuttle, he smiled seeing the project leader standing there proudly with a collection of his workers. Everyone was in clean uniforms or business suits. The bay was clean, the smell of fresh paint still in the air. He took the first few steps from the ladder and extended his hand.

"I am already impressed with the work you all have been doing," he said.

The tall man in the group's front smiled wide and shook the offered hand, "Thank you Director Hawthorn! My people are the best, and take great pride in the work they do."

"Good to finally meet you in person, Mister Wright," Hawthorn said.

He stepped slightly to the side and looked at the two small groups of workers. Each was in a deep blue and white work suit, with bright, clean orange hard hats. Men and women from the colony, dressed for the day's workload, and fully presentable. Deep down he knew it was for show, most workers were very dirty; still this was a source of pride, and it made him smile as well.

He turned and looked up the ladder, seeing the rest of the group coming down. It was time for introductions, so he motioned past the reporters to the commerce minister, "This is Susan Smith, Minister of Commerce for Tronis."

He noted she had on a simple deep blue business suit with a simple button-up shirt. The woman was practical, and that was what he had always admired about her. He had spent the entire flight to the station with his nose in his notes, he hadn't even bothered to see what she had chosen to wear.

While he hoped for more flare, he also considered her simple choice as wise. Given the presence of the work crews, likely the shift leaders in their best work attire, she offered a connection. Once she and Wright shook hands, they spoke quietly, and he was eager to look around the station.

"Um, Director?"

Hawthorn turned his eyes from the landing bay's walls and equipment, seeing Wright giving him a confused look. He glanced and saw the work crew all eyeing the security team coming off the shuttle; three men in military fatigues and one in a sports coat.

"Oh, yes. At the insistence of Deputy Director Hall, I've got a few babysitters," he explained.

"I hadn't expected you to need armed guards on my station sir," Wright said.

Hawthorn waved his hand dismissively, "They'll stay out of the way."

"I have a team of Security officers, if this was that important. I'm sure they would have liked to have been informed at least."

"It's for show, they are only carrying sidearms," Hawthorn said, and he started towards the small doors at the far end of the hangar. "Now, come show me this marvelous station."

"Oh, well, yes sir," Wright said, catching up.

They walked out and down a very basic corridor. A black, slip proof walk with color coded paint strips, and plain gray walls. He was relieved when they eventually came out onto a large promenade that was still in the midst of final work. There were large screens and holo projectors up, a fountain, benches, with octagonal tables and chairs dominating the open floor plan.

"Now this, this is what I expected."

Wright nodded to him, "I'm glad you like it. This will be the heart of the station, allowing people to meet and greet while doing business at shops. The trade offices are going to be over there, in that large room with the bay windows."

"They'll have a commanding view of the place won't they?"

Wright smiled, "Yes, this will be a very personable and lavish location. We'll be the envy of Earth in about a year I suspect."

"That long?" Susan asked.

"Well, we will need to give time for customers to start doing business here, and businesses to shift their storefronts. That will all take some work and effort, as well as investment."

Hawthorn had to admit, it was actually a very optimistic timeline, Earth would counter as well. There would be delays, and many contracts to negotiate. With luck, they could edge Earth out for trade with the larger, non-human nations in a decade. Tronis would become a powerhouse, and likely the center of something greater.

"Shall we see the main conference room?"

Hawthorn nodded, "I think that would be excellent."

Wright led them to an elevator that was tight fitting. The three of them took up most of the space in it, so much so, that only one of the security staff could be with them. He figured the soldiers could take the next one; it wasn't like his assistant was here to be on his case about it.

"The issue I have is the spaceport's dock, if it will be large enough to handle the amount of shipping we need to do," Susan said.

Hawthorn nodded as the lift started to move, "I find I agree, the dock did not appear very large."

"I understand where you're coming from," Wright acknowledged, "but let me offer this alternative: we can manage multiple ships by keeping them in orbit and using a queue system for docking and loading."

Hawthorn made a mental note to study the system the station was going to be putting in place. He would need to present it all in press conferences. A major news outlet reporter from Earth was present on Tronis, maybe they could leverage that to challenge Earth's market dominance early.

He came out of his musing as the lift dinged, "Are you opposed to us bringing more press on the station to demonstrate its functions?"

"Well, Director, I think more attention on this place will be a good thing," Wright said, "but, I have a couple ideas of my own if you'd like to hear them."

"Certainly," Susan said.

Hawthorn nodded as they were led to the conference room. He expected the man had a good mind for it, as he'd been on site overseeing the construction. Clearly, he was a creative type, so why not let him try?

As he stepped through the door into the conference room, he looked around and found himself very disappointed. There were no monitors, or large viewing windows, and as he looked, there were no chairs nor a table.

"What the hell?"

Wright was standing at the door, a firearm pointed at the back of the Security guard's head, "I'm sorry Director, but there is something more important planned for this station."

"What are you talking about?"

"Liberty, our own power? I mean the list is long, however in this case, it's freedom and proper treatment. Earth bleeds the colonies, and the colonies bleed their people. This must end, and it will. Starting here."

"There are soldiers on this station, you can't think you'll be achieving anything," Susan said.

Wright shook his head, and it made Hawthorn's gut tighten. He saw something in the man's eyes, something that told him arguing was not going to work. He recalled seeing it in the eyes of the gamma soldier who had been in his office before.

"What do you want, Mister Wright?" Hawthorn asked.

When Susan looked at him, he just shook his head and held up his hand. He wanted it clear to the man with the gun, there would be no trouble. He didn't want Wright to think he needed to harm someone to get his point across.

"The same as you, the prosperity of Tronis. Earth's soldiers gone, along with one additional thing," Wright said, "our independence. Specifically, that of the people, not just the elite."

"What are you talking about?" Susan asked.

"Ask him," Wright said.

Hawthorn felt confused, there was no oppression on Tronis, there was a poverty issue, but this was going to help that. Create new jobs, and opportunities.

"I have no idea what you mean by that, there is no elite class on Tronis, that's why the founders established it!""

"And yet the troubles of the old world still plague us!" Wright snapped.

"Everyday people go hungry! Our pleas are ignored, and you go on as things are just fine; you even brought Earth military here to kill our people!"

"They were here to rescue those taken by," Hawthorn realized something was wrong, "oh God, you are part of that pirate group!"

"Freedom fighters!"

"You nearly starved our people by attacking trade ships! Of course, Earth sent soldiers!" Susan screamed.

Hawthorn reached for her arm, but was too late. Wright shot her twice with a second firearm he hadn't seen. The guard's face shook him, displaying a look of utter failure. Upon further examination, he noticed that his side arm had been used.

"Now then," Wright started, taking a deep breath, "you two will be staying here. I'll have your security rounded up shortly."

As soon as the door slid shut, Hawthorn was on his knees next to Susan, as was his security officer. The man looked at him and shook his head; Hawthorn felt his stomach drop. He had known Susan since she arrived on Tronis, she was driven, but always had the best in mind.

He put his suit coat over her and stood slowly, not sure what to do at this point. He paced, looking at the empty room, trying to imagine he was in his office. If he could think, maybe he could figure this out. If nothing else, he needed to understand Wright's motives clearly enough to open a meaningful dialogue.

The first few passes brought Susan's body into view, breaking his thoughts with the horrible present. He amended his route, always turning away from her, allowing him to think and not break down. He spared one glance and saw his bodyguard was already doing an exploration of the room.

He nodded to himself, that was a good sign, the man was a go getter, he knew to be active and do his job. The energy fit the situation, and allowed him a better atmosphere to think in. If they were both working on the problem, maybe they'd solve it.

"What's the protocol if we miss a check in?"

The officer stopped his exploration, "Well, first they'd try one of the other coms, either to the station or to the transport ship."

"Then what?"

The man shrugged, "Likely they'd deviate the escorts back to check in."

Hawthorn nodded and started to pace again, rubbing his chin as he walked. The entire process would take time, and being a bureaucrat, he knew how long a process could take. It would take perhaps an hour to get things moving and send help. The militia would send a ship with a small contingent of soldiers expecting trouble.

"Sir," the other man interrupted, "it's likely that they want the Security Office to contact the station. That would open up a channel for them to start making demands."

"You think they want to go directly to that?"

The man nodded. "I think so, they'll want to make demands while people are confused and not acting."

"Being a hostage taker part of your job qualifications?"

The man chuckled and Hawthorn felt better. The joke felt rude, but he had gotten the sense it was a good fit to the man's personality. He was direct, and experienced, that likely meant he had a dark sense of humor.

"No sir, but I have been trained in these sorts of situations, even wrote some of the response plans. That seems like the most likely game plan at the moment."

Hawthorn nodded. "Till we know more."

6

Eversley checked the latch on the last duffle bag he sat in the transport's harness. He had all the equipment the team would likely need to respond to anyone calling for help. Once satisfied, he secured the locker and took one more look over the transport, poring over what might be missing.

"You aren't going to will it into existence brother," came Keith's voice behind him.

Eversley laughed, "Well, I thought I'd try."

"How's that working for you?"

Eversley shrugged, "Oh, about as well as you'd think. Everything ready in your corner?"

Keith nodded, "Yeah, Granberg is doing his final checks now too. You good?"

Eversley nodded, "Yep. Gear is stowed, minus whatever the fuck I'm forgetting. Team is all geared up and Holte is doing an inspection."

"So, you're all five by five then?"

Eversley looked at him for a long time and then nodded, "I'm good man."

"Alright, I just figured I'd check, this has been the longest you've been gone from home since the divorce. How's your boy taking it?"

"He's at my mom's place, having the time of his life right now. Playing kickball even."

Holte's voice broke in, "I thought we agreed, no home talk when we were out."

Eversley smiled and laughed, "She's got you there Chief."

"Well, technically we aren't outside the wire so, doesn't count," Keith countered.

"If you say so buddy."

"I do say so," Keith said with a smile. "You two have to realize, it's not just in the thick of it I need to be worrying about you. The time in between, and what's going on at home are just as important to the moments out here."

Eversley nodded, "I know man, just not a common thing in the Space Corps. I appreciate it though."

"At least one of you does," Keith said as he looked at Holte.

Holte chuckled, "Oh I get it, I just like giving you hell."

"On that note, how's Andrea taking your deployment?"

Holte shrugged, "About how you'd expect. It was our anniversary when you called, don't ya know?"

Eversley laughed, he had heard all about it on the trip to Tronis. Holte had her girlfriend's favorite meal made, wine found, and perfume. They had just sat down to eat when the call came in, and apparently Keith was called some creative names the rest of the evening.

It was something he admitted he liked about Keith though, he never left the bad news delivery to others. Most would have left it to the logistic section and put out fires at the base. Keith made sure to be the one giving the news, as well as put out the fire. It led to more than one nasty argument but, in the end, he had to admit, it made him respect Keith more. He wasn't just an excellent shooter, he was a caring team leader.

"Besides," Keith's laugh broke his internal thoughts, "I've had your cooking. I probably did her a favor."

"Hey now! That's hitting below the belt."

Holte was laughing as well. Eversley shook his head in wonder at it, he and Holte were close friends, but Keith seemed to have some special liberties. If anyone else would have made that comment, Holte would have them in a submission hold.

"Seriously though," Keith said, "I look to both of you to take over at some point; not just at the fire team level."

"Planning on taking Jubes' job do you?" Holte asked with a smirk.

Keith shook his head, "Not exactly, but eventually I'll promote, and I'll need good team leaders."

They laughed and exchanged fist bumps, sharing the moment and smiling. Deployments didn't have enough of this sort of interaction as far as Eversley was concerned. All the work that went into what they were doing seemed to pile up. Nights out having drinks and cards had their place but genuine moments were rare.

"Alright, I'll leave you two to it. I've got my mess to get sorted," Keith said.

"Yeah, you better make sure Granberg is reading the tags and not eating them!"

Keith laughed and waved at them as he stepped out of the lander. Once he was out of sight, Eversley looked at Holte. She wasn't looking his way, she was watching Keith go, her hands on her hips.

"What's up?"

Holte looked back to him, "I dunno, you see Keith as the command type?"

"Maybe," Eversley offered, "I mean he's spent enough time training us. People don't operate forever, sooner or later they end up the old guys."

"Could be," she said, "You think he's looking to leave?"

"Could be, his kids are getting older, he's missed a lot. Anyway, what am I forgetting? I've looked all over this lander and can't figure out what's missing."

Holte laughed and took his tablet so she could double check. They started at the front of the transport and worked their way towards the back. They checked each piece of gear, each bag, and each harness again. Eversley was thinking he was just worrying too much, till Holte held up a duffle.

"You forgot your bag dude."

Eversley shook his head, "Fuck too."

Before he could prepare a defense, the klaxon started sounding for the base. Eversley stepped out the back of the lander and saw flight crews pouring out of the buildings across from them. He looked up and listened to the announcement that followed the alarm.

"All flight crews to stations! Emergency! Clear all Tiger Sharks for takeoff!"

Eversley watched the crew wheeling out the attack craft. It was like watching someone put food on an ant colony. Little specs started crawling all over the food in a matter of moments, breaking it down and hauling it away. This was quite the reverse, and equally enthralling.

As they moved the Tiger Sharks into place, crews rushed up with carts carrying weapon pods, then started attaching them, changing out yellow flags for green ones. Eversley wasn't sure what each uniform color meant, but there were at least four different crews around each craft.

One man in a red uniform was carrying a tablet and overseeing the operation. That part he could sus out easily enough; that one was making all the calls. As he called out, hands went up from one color or another, eventually all of them falling away to rush off to another Tiger Shark.

"What the hell?" Holte asked behind him.

Eversley shook his head, "Drill maybe? Pirate attack?"

"None of those," came Keith's voice.

Eversley glanced over and saw the chief coming over with a Tronis Militia lieutenant on his heels. The woman couldn't have been out of her teens. She had a fierce look though, and he figured she had at least put in the work to earn the bars.

"I need this troop transport unloaded right now," she barked.

Keith looked over at her with a look Eversley had seen a time or two himself. He'd earned it when he got upset with Holte one day in training. He and Keith called the same place home, and he knew the man's reputation, in that moment he knew it was undersold. Keith had spent an hour making him do drills and chewing him out, he almost pitied the young lieutenant in that moment. Almost.

"I was pretty sure I said I'd handle it, Lieutenant Wright," Keith said flatly.

Lieutenant Wright stiffened some and her eyes were wide, "This is a local matter, and you are in my way. Now, get this bird cleared out!"

"Find somewhere else to be! It'll be ready before your weekend warriors are geared up!"

The two stood their locking eyes, Eversley nudged Holte with his elbow and motioned back inside. She nodded, and pulled out a small tablet of her own, pressing a few keys as she walked back in. Eversley looked back over at the building they were using as a barracks, and as expected, both fire teams poured out the door.

"We'll have it cleared out Chief, do they want both or just the one?" Eversley asked.

"Just the one," Keith answered sharply.

"Any of your gear left on here I'll consider Tronis Militia property, make sure you get it all," Lieutenant Wright said.

The woman spun on her heel and stalked off to a different building. Once everyone moved past him up the ramp to start the unload, Eversley stepped out to Keith. He was still staring after the woman and, if he didn't know any better, growling.

"Taking after Granberg a bit, are ya?"

Keith glanced back and shook his head, "Next time the UNSC wants to send support to the colonies they can Send Alpha Squadron."

"I'm not a fan of the colonials either man, but it won't help our situation if you eat their troops."

Keith laughed and nodded, "Maybe, but I'd feel better."

"What's going on?"

"Something happened on the new trade station they built. No one is saying a lot, which is good operational security."

Eversley smiled, "Well, they got that going for them."

"That's about all. You've seen these militia soldiers, they aren't trained for a serious fight. That's why a full third of our team is strung out around Tronis and the system, watching them to be sure they don't get killed sweeping up these terrorists."

Eversley shrugged, "Well, we can't hold their hand the whole time. I mean she didn't run off from you so, that's something."

"Maybe," Keith said, "how long to unload?"

Eversley checked the growing stack of equipment, "Two minutes."

"Good. They'll be out in about ten I bet."

"Want us to wash and wax it?"

Keith laughed again, "Naw, I'd hate for them to expect it all the time."

Eversley laughed and moved to help everyone, although it looked like there was almost too much inside the lander. Holte had them in a chain, moving things out. He went to work sorting and stacking the growing pile of equipment and gear.

As he figured, the two-minute window was spot on; the last of the gear was out, and they left all the storage areas open. He prioritized and staged things so they could move them back to the barracks.

"So," Keith said as he stepped over, "did you figure out what you were missing?"

"Don't start with me," Eversley laughed in response.

Keith smirked, but it faded as he snapped to attention, causing Eversley to turn and follow suit. Commander Jubert was standing there with the UNIS Major they had seen earlier. He felt a pit grow in his stomach at the trouble this probably meant was coming.

"As you were," Jubert said as he moved past the team.

Eversley set to work getting the rest of the squadron moving the gear back to the barracks. However, he kept his ear open. It wasn't exactly forbidden, nor advised, but they had a habit of keeping tabs on what was happening around them. It made life easier for everyone up and down the chain.

"Colonial Director Hawthorn was taken hostage about an hour ago," Jubert said.

Keith nodded, "Alright, so that explains all the sudden activity, what's our role?"

Major Shaikh spoke first, "For the moment, we have no official role. That said, I want your team to do an assessment on the best way to take the space station and execute a rescue."

"The colonial forces will be affecting the rescue," explained Jubert.

Keith nodded, "Alright, are they up for this?"

Commander Jubert and Major Shaikh both shook their heads. Eversley had to resist the urge to swear aloud. The last bag was ready, so he took it and left the conversation behind. Once the door closed behind him, he tossed the bag onto a table and went to Holte.

"Chief is going to be asking us to get a plan to do a breach and rescue operation on the trade station."

Holte looked at him and blinked, "You were eavesdropping again, weren't you?"

Eversley shrugged, "Only a little."

"Fine," Holte said, "alright everyone listen up! I need a holo projector found, get the tables set up for a planning session!"

7

John moved to the side after they set the table up, and the hologram of the space station was floating in the middle of the room. He set his camera up and started to film the team as they were doing the work of planning and evaluating. It was fascinating to see, and he knew his viewers would love it; the look of how things went together before an operation.

Holte, Keith, Eversley, and Granberg were standing around the hologram with tablets, and he noticed each of them were marking places on the map. Red squares, blue circles, and shaded boxes started appearing in different places. He made a few notes on his tablet to ask them what they were doing, that way he could narrate the process later.

Colonel Shaikh came in with Commander Jubert a few moments later, John made sure to keep his presence minimal. The intelligence officer clearly had no want for his presence, and he was not about to give the man any more reason to remove him from filming the team. There was a quiet exchange between the two of them and Keith, then a better map of the station appeared in the holographic projector.

"Alright," Keith called out, "circle up!"

John debated putting two camera drones up along with his point of view camera as the room came to life. Chairs were being brought over, and the remaining two fire teams were now in a circle around the projection. Eversley, Holte, and Granberg took their seats, leaving one open for Keith who stayed standing with Jubert and Shaikh.

"Heads in the game folks," he said, "approximately two and a half hours ago, insurgents took Colonial Director Hawthorn hostage on Avalon station. There is an unknown number of them, but if we assume all the workers on the station at the time of his arrival are in on this, that puts the number in the area of one hundred armed fighters."

Granberg raised his hand, "Are these guys in with the group we took out when we first got here?"

Shaikh nodded, "That would appear to be the case," he motioned to a face that appeared on the holo next to the station. "This is the head engineer overseeing the station, James Wright. His name came up in the data recovered from the raid you conducted three days ago."

Everyone nodded, and John thought he saw Eversley's eyes narrow. In the same instance, his hand shot up, along with the rest of his body. He took half a step towards the hologram and was reaching for Keith's tablet.

"Hey," he said, "wasn't that Lieutenant's name Wright?"

Keith nodded, "Yep. I've already voiced the concern."

"Lieutenant Wright," Shaikh said, "has undergone vetting; she and her brother have been estranged for three years now. There has been no contact between them. Apparently, her enlisting in the Tronis Militia upset him greatly."

"Deputy Director Ball has signed off on this as well," said Jubert. "She and the lieutenant are acquainted and feels the best chance to resolve this peacefully, is to give her the chance to challenge her brother over his actions."

There was a shaking of heads and muttering from the team, and John felt he agreed. It made no sense to him, in fact, it sounded like a terrible idea. John felt it'd be like asking his own father to come to a family dinner; he could imagine how angry he would be. The service was a source of hard problems in his family, and he couldn't imagine it being any different for the Wrights.

"There is also the other problem of logistics," Jubert was saying, "the bulk of the militia is out all over the sector and is radio silent at the moment."

"Getting ready to facilitate a large-scale take down," added Keith.

Everyone nodded, and John saw the resignation in their faces. There was no one else the militia could send into the fight. That made the situation what it was, the militia had to use the people they had.

"Are we going to be in on this action?" Qureshi asked.

Keith shook his head, "Not at the moment."

"I want your team to build a plan for the militia," Sheikh said, "You all have more experience in the field, more specialized training, and to be honest, are far more competent."

John blinked. *Did that man just give someone a compliment and mean it?*

"What kind of time frame do we have?" Holte asked.

Keith held up two fingers, "Two hours. That's the flight time between here and Avalon Station."

Everyone in the circle of chairs nodded, pulled out tablets, and started reading something. Keith was walking around putting new markers on the map, green arrows. John watched it on his tablet through the cameras, it somehow made it easier to conceive his words for the story; seeing what his viewers would see.

A shadow fell across his screen, "Hello Colonel, something I can do for you?"

"Just making sure you are doing as told," Shaikh said.

"I'm sticking to the guidelines of my contract with the Space Corps," John added.

"To what angle?"

John looked up and sat his tablet aside, "The truth. The only way people can make wise decisions is by being properly informed."

"Yes, the call of the media," Shaikh said. "We tell the truth, so long as it suits the agency agenda."

"Sounds a bit more like the intelligence service mantra."

"You are suggesting our paths are not dissimilar?"

"No," John said, "they are each other's antithesis. I spread information, you try to sequester it."

Shaikh made a motion of weighing something between both hands, "We both have our audience to cater to, no?"

"That's what you took from that?"

"Well, think of it this way," Shaikh said, "you must please a producer who wants to sell the story. I must please officers who make decisions based on what I provide them."

"Except I don't leave things out to suit my needs."

Shaikh shook his head, "I leave out what is irrelevant to a decision. The officers are interested in understanding the risk, casualty possibilities, effects of inaction, effects of action, and the recommended force for the desired effect. All the details important to provide the information to plan and decide. You feel the public needs to know all the parts to decide as well? To claim they would have done it better or differently? Many without the lens of experience? Does a grocery store manager need to know all the information that went into the choice to kill a terrorist leader? Would they even understand the thought process?"

"They should know what is going on in their world! Why the politicians and military make the choices they do!"

"And live in fear every day? They do not have a wider view, and to be honest, the amount of information going into those sorts of actions would make for boring news stories. That is why the media grips tightest on the most reactive parts of a story. You want the viewer and reader to be hooked, interested, and invested."

John shifted in his seat, "They need to know the truth of matters."

"You may gather the truth," Shaikh said, "but not all makes the news. It is the story that gets people pinned to your producer's idea. You may not like the version of the world I represent, but do not think we are dissimilar in motive."

"Only in the desired result," John said flatly.

Shaikh shrugged and turned towards the door, "I would say in the amount of truth that gets to our audiences."

John watched the man leave and suppressed a shudder. In the best of times, he disliked officers like the colonel, having one leering over his work made it worse. He briefly entertained the idea of posting a part of the story featuring the man, but thought better of it. The colonel would review every scrap of data he tried to send out, it wouldn't make it out of the facility.

"Entry here is likely the best," Holte was saying.

John refocused on the camera and the team; that was his priority. It took only a few moments to get the camera drones in place to record the discussion. Holte pointed to a section on the surface of the station that, according to the plans, was newly finished.

"A team can get into the superstructure here and make their way to an access point in the corridors."

Keith stepped over and was eyeing the route she had outlined. His finger traced along the route until it met the interior halls. He tapped on a section that was in an isolated part of the hall, no doors were near it and the exit led to the hangar section.

"You're looking to secure the transport and move from there?"

Holte nodded, "Yep, should be a token force there to keep in on the station. I'd say to use in their own exit, if things go bad. Militia could use it as an ambush site depending on how the situation is evolving."

"Looks like a wise move."

"No joy," Granberg said.

Keith and Holte moved over to Granberg who was holding up his tablet.

"None of the militia present have passed zero atmospheric qualifications," he said, "there is no way to be sure they'd even be able to make the space walk through the unfinished section."

Keith nodded, and Holte swore.

"Alright, give me an alternative entry point that gets the team to the hangar."

Holte stood looking at the hologram, "It would mean going loud. Either the lander parks on top and they breach the hull, or they blast their way into the hangar."

"Puts the hostages at risk, gives the bad guys plenty of warning," Keith said.

Holte nodded, "Yep. Okay, scratch that."

Keith patted her on the shoulder and moved over to another group as she and Granberg started to review the layout again. John moved one drone to follow him and peek over his shoulder. He had to suppress a smile at how good the footage looked while Keith approached Silverling, Andrews, and Bekele.

"Any intel on the station we can work with?"

Silverling shook her head, "Nope. We don't have the signal strength to access the station's computer network for a hack."

Keith nodded, "How about external?"

"Tiger Sharks are about an hour out yet," Andrews said. "I think I'll get a couple passes before the lander gets there with the weekend warriors."

"Militia."

"Right, that's what I said, Chief."

John had to suppress a chuckle, he was aware of Andrew's humor, and it was nice to see it aimed at someone else. He had a few pointed comments when John had first arrived and made the foolish mistake of running into the morgue. The man was relentless, even in the battle on the moon station, he was poking at the fact John had vomited.

Keith and the drone moved on to another cluster of the team that was sitting around a smaller hologram of the station. Red dots and squares were all over the station's representation. John looked up from the screen to see if he could understand it better directly. It didn't help.

"So, how is the opposition planning going?"

Qureshi looked up from her work and gave a slight inclination of her head. The other two, Harrison and Turgenev stayed busy plotting the potential enemy ambush locations.

They glanced up and then at her as they tapped a few more keys moving their mock defense forces.

"If I were them," she said, "and knew this station inside and out, I would consolidate in the administration tower."

Keith leaned over and looked at their notes, "Why?"

"Visibility for one," she said. "It's in the center of the large pavilion they are so proud of. Any attackers would have to run a gauntlet of set up ambushes."

"Leaving you with all the time in the galaxy to off a hostage and make a point."

"If not kill them all, or the attackers."

"I don't think they have enough training for that," Keith said, "but any fool can set up an ambush."

8

The holographic emitters hummed to life, the live feed from the militia unit taking shape as they sat in the lander. Eversley noticed they had already dawned their combat helmets and were preparing weapons. He liked the idea they were being so efficient and glanced at Holte who nodded.

The audio came on next, thankfully it was clear so he could hear the typical idle chatter, the nervous tone in voices that proceeded action. Things seemed to be about as he expected, the unit was disciplined, and he was glad for that, but they weren't as disciplined as he would have preferred. It was the cost though, they had to get this experience somehow.

"We are ninety seconds from landing," Wright said.

Eversley glanced at the holographic feed of the station, seeing the live feed from the Tiger Sharks as they made their passes. He could see the lander making contact with the surface of the station where they had planned, finally settling on an area that was designated for office space, and far enough away from the main tower and probable defensive line.

Sparks drew his attention back to the feed as the team was making a cut in the station's hull; it took them two minutes to cut through the outer hull and lift the plate up. The next section to cut through took less time, and the third that would give access to the room, took only thirty seconds.

"Making entry," Wright said.

One by one the militia team lowered themselves into the room. The first two checked the corridor beyond and gave a thumbs up. It took another two minutes, and the entire squad was in the station, where they secured the outer hull plate to prevent decompression.

"Alright, you lot," Wright said, "we are in it now. Remember the plan. Remember to breathe."

Eversley was sure he heard a collective exhale over the coms at that. He briefly thought back to his first breaching exercise, when Keith had said almost the same thing to him. In every training exercise he would say, "breath controlled everything, and thus to do well, you had to breathe."

"Move out!"

Eversley looked around the room and noticed all the team was glued to the holograms. Their faces bathed in the soft glow of the emitters, a counter to the darkness that seemed more intense around them. They were in the moment as much as the militia who were physically there could have been. He had to admit even he felt the dryness in his mouth and the change in his heartbeat.

The militia moved forward in relative unison, stepping in rhythm with one another, as they cleared each room. They selected the corridor, as it was unimportant, and took a roundabout route to the main plaza. There was also the catch, it had none of the internal system monitoring equipment in place yet. That made the infiltration invisible. It also meant there was nowhere to tap into the system.

"I'd feel better about this if there was overwatch, Chief," Eversley said.

Keith nodded, "I know, but this is the best case now. If they find an access to tie into when they make the commons, they'll take it."

Eversley looked over and gave him a dubious look, the target fixation would be too great. The militia unit would put all their energy into the engagement with the separatists and the hostage situation. They just weren't used to star base assaults.

"I've got movement ahead!"

Eversley felt his heart skip, and his eyes focused on the holographic image again. He scanned all the images for whoever called out, then settled on one who was looking back towards the team and then down a hall.

"Where?" Came Wright's voice.

"Just down this hall, near the third office," said the soldier.

Eversley didn't know any of them, and he regretted that. He made a point to learn them after this, making training and cooperations easier. There was also the fact it would make sitting on the sidelines like this easier.

"Alright," Wright said, "Harkens, Carter, you two get up here."

She motioned in the direction they had shown her. Conversation gave way to hand signals and the small ad hoc fire team moved down the hall. Once to the first door, Wright signaled and two of the four moved around the door carefully.

Eversley watched as she used her hand and the rifle to signal how they would open and clear the room. The instant the door opened, he flinched as they immediately went in and moved their rifles around to clear the room. *Far too fast, and no caution.*

The room was empty. He let out a sigh of relief as they moved forward to the next, repeating the process again, faster this time, and more so for the next. Eversley felt his skin crawling; too much was happening, in too short a time.

"They need to slow the fuck down," Eversley grumbled aloud.

Keith nodded, "I agree, it'll hit them soon, if they don't open a door into a fight."

The group finally moved up to the last door; the one he expected to have trouble in it. As the door slid open, the cameras showed the inside of the room, then panned back and forth showing there was nothing there.

"You sure you saw something?" Wright said.

The soldier nodded, "Yes Ma'am."

Eversley looked at Holte, then looked over to Keith, who was already on his way to Jubert. He looked back at the images from the other soldiers and looked for anything out of the ordinary. The corridors all seemed empty, no movement, just empty dark halls.

"Where the hell are they?"

"Dude, I don't know, but I know I saw something!"

Eversley shook his head, "Learn some radio etiquette, dammit," he muttered to the holograms.

His comment went unnoticed, clearly unheard by the militia soldiers, as they continued to chatter amid themselves on the situation. He didn't fault them too much. Chatter about who saw what and where was normal, however, the amount they were talking was beyond what he ever felt comfortable with. One or two jabs, then back on mission.

"We can't keep chasing ghosts," Wright said. "It's chewing up time. We need to get to the tower and secure the director."

The militia nodded and reformed their section, moving back on the designated path Eversley had helped plot out. They moved through the rest of the section with caution, checking the halls, and ignoring the offices down them. Eversley did note, they would deploy Proximity and directed devices to secure the passages though.

The pavilion came into view, finally, as the unit came to a halt. Wright gave the signal to spread out, and the militia started moving towards concealing positions. Their movements became slower, more methodical, more to Eversley's liking.

"Slow and steady, guys," he muttered.

He felt the disconnection from the real world happening as the situation drew him into the holograms. He found that he focused on a singular hologram, probably because they took his typical position in a formation. The familiar feelings in his body started, even the prickle on his skin.

Slowly and carefully, the militia moved from position to position, creeping towards the objective. Eversley noticed the absurdity of the central pavilion, the tall tower-like structure, was more art than function; something tall and massive in the open space of the promenade. It made the situation tactically nightmarish.

Every open balcony or window on it was a potential observation point for the enemy, high above the open scant cover of the half-built promenade, it could even be easily defended. That was the problem, he decided, even the most basic individual knew they'd have the advantage of the high ground there.

He noticed the militia kept their weapons aimed up, as much as out and around them, as they moved. It was the best practice, and despite the disagreement on the path, he had to admit, they were being as careful as possible about it. The more he looked at the structure, the more he worried; it almost seemed purposely built for the situation. Seeing it on the maps was one thing, to see the image, made his skin crawl.

"Keith,"

Just as his friend turned to answer, chaos erupted on the holograms. Shots rang out, screams and call outs came from every hologram as the militia came under fire. Everyone in the observation room twitched, jarred out of the immersion by the fire and the instinct to take cover, countered by their sense of place.

"Fire left! Fire left!"

Eversley watched as Lieutenant Wright took control of her team and started getting the situation in hand. She reformed the squad into a defensive position and started to take a long look at the situation. He was still absorbed in the holograms, but he heard his fellow team members trying to make sense of chaos.

"Close the gaps," Wright said.

She was getting the militia soldiers moving and making a controlled withdrawal from the promenade. Soldiers moved from cover to cover, laying down weapons fire to let others move to safety. The entire process took less time than it felt like it did, but still too long.

Eversley watched three holograms go dark, and two just showing the floor. The militia had lost a full quarter of their strength in the opening shots, Not planning on a quick reaction force was hurting the situation as well. *Damn the arrogant fools.*

"Cover here," Wright called, pointing at the half-built security checkpoint to the promenade.

Two soldiers took position and started covering the rest of the team's retreat. As far as he could see, the shooting was coming from various positions around the promenade. Eversley let out a breath of relief. The high ground would have ended the team.

"Take positions, get control of the fight," Wright encouraged her shooters.

Wright turned to fire and give another order, only for that soldier to get hit and stop moving. She swore and called for aid as another took position beside her. Laser fire, bullets, and even plasma bounced off their cover.

"Fire team one to Homebase," Write called over the radio.

Again, Eversley had to give her credit for her controlled voice. She was matter of fact, a bit amped due to her adrenalin, but he was more than willing to give that a pass.

"Homebase," came the response, "what's your situation?"

"We are taking highly accurate and concentrated fire. I've got six down hard, three more wounded."

"Understood. Alternate extraction point, Lambda. Can you get to it?"

There was a long pause while Wright turned and fired at a position. After a few shots, her view panned, looking at her position and the state of her team, receiving thumbs up from some. She brought the map up on her HUD, and the line from their position to the designated point came up.

"A-firm," she said, "Beginning fall back."

Eversley let out a breath and nodded to himself as he watched Wright give the orders to fall back. It was orderly, careful, and blessedly, the militia soldiers had enough sense to stay concealed as they moved out.

Once Wright was clear of the position, she tossed a smoke grenade out. While it would do nothing to anyone in the area, it made following them far riskier. The idea being that if you can't see what you are walking into, you won't be keen to do it.

The team was falling back down the same corridor, but instead of going back to the original entry point, they took a right and went down a different hall. Eversley winced as they didn't bother clearing the offices they moved by.

In one hologram, Eversley saw a door slide open. Instinctively, he gave a warning call, but he wasn't on their com line. The soldier didn't see it, and they gave no call as a round device rolled into the hall.

The next moments were a blur, several holograms blinked off, some scrambled and tumbled, others just showed the floor. All he could hear were disoriented shouts and sporadic weapons fire; the scene had him frozen in place. After a few moments, there were no more weapons fired.

"Don't," Wright's voice came faintly, though not from her hologram, it wasn't playing.

Eversley looked back and forth, trying to find a camera with a view of what was happening. There, in the blue glow of the hologram, stood someone in dark combat armor, with a rifle leveled at the face of Lieutenant Wright. She was laying against a wall, one of her soldiers laid across her in a failed attempt to protect her from the grenade.

Soon others came into view, men and women holding rifles, wearing gray work suits. One knelt and Eversley was looking for footage with their face, he found it and winced. Wright's brother was the one kneeling.

"I told you what would happen if you tried to stop this," he hissed.

Wright worked a few times to speak, "And I thought you had better sense. How many innocent people are going to die now because you didn't want to put effort into getting a better life?"

The man shouted and struck her with a wrench, screaming over and over as he did so. It set off a flurry of actions as the other workers seemed to be caught in the same moment of rage. Screams of anger, mixed with screams of pain, could be heard as the frenzy happened.

After it subsided, the ones in combat suits were still, weapons pointed at the others. Eversley thought that any moment another battle would erupt between the two groups; there was no such instance. The ones in the work suits looked around and then walked away, all except one.

"This one was of your pride?" asked the armored figure next to him.

He nodded, "My sister."

"Nothing is more painful,"

"It's the price we must pay!"

Eversley shook his head in disbelief. Everyone thought that Wright's family connection would give the man pause, instead, it only seemed to ignite a terrible rage in the man. He started to shake visibly, then strode off out of camera view.

The armored soldier, still standing there, looked the way he went before turning to offer a salute to someone unseen. Eversley felt his blood chill when he recognized the salute. Then, the soldier took off the combat helmet, revealing the face underneath. Soft tan fur, with ruddy hints around the cheek and a wide, firm jaw. Ears that were oval shaped, sitting higher on the head than a human's would.

"Holy fuck," he said aloud. "Shezlan."

9

John watched the screen go dark, just as the others had, and felt the acid taste come back to him. He struggled to find focus, then decided on the old standby, recording the events unfolding around him. His fingers quickly brushed the control pad on his arm, bringing up the drone camera, and the disconnection from the event with it.

"Holy fuck," Holte breathed.

The remainder of the team was stunned into silence, eyes locked on the feed, and the people moving around the bodies of the militia force. Each face bore some manner of shock and anger, some stared in disbelief. Those, John knew, were trying to understand the latest development. Death was normal, but to see the enemy step into the light so fully, it was like the boogeyman come to life!

"Everyone," Keith said, "get your heads in the game. Time the varsity showed them how it's done. Saddle up."

The room burst into motion as each member of the squadron moved to their already prepared bags and started to gear up. It occurred to John how convenient it was to have their gear prepared, but he also gave thought to what they were supposed to be doing. They expected something to happen eventually, just not during a hostage situation.

John watched Keith and Jubert talk in the corner and thought briefly about putting his drone over to listen in on them. The look Jubert gave him told him not to. *Did the man hear his thoughts?*

He decided it was better not asking and went back to documenting the team getting geared up. There had not been such a chance to see them transform from the laughing, jovial group to the hardened operators they were renowned for. Knowing that such an opportunity couldn't be wasted, he had his drone roaming, capturing the scene.

Everyone had stripped down to their under suit, a black, almost soft material, that served as the liner for their full body armor. John thought it looked, and felt, like wearing long Johns during the winter. Each part of the armor went on from the boots up, section by section.

Eversley and Granberg seemed the most professional about it, each piece being checked and rechecked before locking into place. John suspected the two had a minor sort of rivalry going between them, who was best? As far as John was concerned, that was Keith, but he'd be hard pressed to pick anyone for third place. Holte was clearly Keith's second; John would bet a year's salary on that.

When the camera panned over Silverling's face, John had to blink. In the time since the events on the asteroid, he had gotten used to the lighthearted woman she was, out of the armor. The stony expression he saw on her face gave the idea that was the real her, and the happy card player was just a mask.

"Newsie," Stewart called, "get over here and get suited."

John blinked, "I–I don't think I'm going to be allowed to tag along big man."

"Well, till we know for sure, you need to kit up, and just so you aren't just dead weight, you'll be carrying my rescue packs."

John nodded, "Yes sir."

His last run in with the medic had already taught him there was no space to refuse. As far as Stewart was concerned, he needed a pack animal and Newsie fit the bit. John didn't know whether he should feel flattered or worried, but that was just how life was.

"I'll have you packing six of these, since you won't have the extra weight of ammo and hardware."

John nodded again as he slid the pack into the backpack-mounting he was handed; it clearly marked the hard armored case to designate medical supplies. He thought that it would be simple to recognize when someone needed it, but he had been informed that traditionally a medic was seen as a 'noncombatant' and should be spared direct fire. If the aliens ever decided to honor that rule, remained uncertain.

"Anything you want me to be doing while this goes on?"

Stewart shook his head, "Nope, you just stay with Andrews and when I yell, you two haul ass."

"I'm still not carrying your gear, man," said Andrews.

"Yeah, yeah," said Stewart.

John chuckled some then looked back at his footage, the rest of the team was suited up and checking weapons now. He decided he needed to do the same, and with Stewart's help he got the equipment on. It occurred to him that in this small moment, there was no outward difference between him and the rest of gamma. *Well, minus a weapon.* He reminded himself, but he wasn't there to fight, he was there to document a story, and this one was going to be over the top.

He recalled his drone and mounted it on the side of his medical backpack. Loading and testing the capacitors on the rifles wasn't exactly the footage he needed; there was enough of that in his stock file. John flinched at the audible clacking sound as they added more emergency medical tools to his armor's carry supports.

"I should have asked for a helper years ago," Stewart said.

"Oh, funny," John said as someone put the last piece of equipment on.

"Alright," Keith said, "Helmets on, Coms check."

John did as the others did and waited for the armor to power up; which only took seconds. The heads-up display filled his field of view and faded when he focused on things past it. Soon he heard all the squad individually reply to Keith's callsigns.

Most were generic, he noted; one-one, one-two, two-one, two-two, and so forth. Then, he called others out, Mama Bear, Pew-Pew, Super Hero, Doc, Heavy, and finally, Newsie. John blinked at the name, and it took Keith calling it again, for him to give the return his signal was good.

"Figure the com out a little faster next time."

"Yes sir," John said.

John felt a nudge in his side, Stewart was looking at him mouthing the words 'Don't call him sir.'

He blanched at himself, he knew Keith long enough to know better than to do that. The stress and the flow of action just let it fall out. He was sure Keith wouldn't get too worried about it, but one thing he had learned about the military, be careful who you call sir.

"Alright," Jubert called out, "we will be going with the original plan they had us concoct, entry via space walk to the hangar. Two elements will deploy. I'll stay on overwatch on the ship. Rules of engagement are simple in this instance; Every being on that station is now considered hostile. Primary concern is Director Hawthorn's safety. You kill everything between you and that goal; human and alien alike."

Everyone nodded in agreement, they had already drilled the plan even though the militia had to take a different approach. It was good exercise and Keith liked to keep plans handy in case of a misfire, which was surely the case now. John was still trying to catch up mentally, so it was good he watched them drill. He at least knew what was about to happen.

The door opened and John felt his stomach fall. Colonel Shaikh came striding in looking around, and, for once, seemed surprised. He looked around the room quickly and then moved towards Keith and Jubert. John almost sent his drone, then had a different idea, and darkened his visor.

"I take it you are already aware of what has happened," Shaikh said, "as well as what comes next?"

Jubert nodded, "Right on both counts, Colonel. We already have a plan developed and are ready to go."

"Your team is up to this?"

Keith looked at everyone, then back to the colonel, "There's no one more up for this than my team, sir. We've got it."

"I have your transport already cleared for takeoff, at your pleasure, gentlemen."

Keith looked at Granberg and nodded.

"Alright everybody," Granberg said, "roll out!"

John felt himself caught up in the frenzy as the team stood at attention a moment and then moved for the doorway. They all formed into a single line, stepping in rhythm, and John found it was catchy, stepping in time with the others. He was behind Stewart, and in front of Andrews; both men making him feel small, even if Andrews wasn't much more than his height.

The chain moved past the Colonel, Keith, and Jubert, when he overheard a small bit of the conversation.

"Something else, Colonel?" Keith asked.

"No," Shiekh replied, "just looking for someone I wanted some words with."

"Well, happy hunting," Jubert said, motioning Keith to follow him.

John allowed himself a small smile and had to keep from laughing. He expected the Colonel to be there to make him stay on base and not deploy with the team. He recalled their earlier talk and knew he wouldn't specifically hold him, but he would certainly delay him long enough to miss the transport.

The man could split rules just as well as anyone John had ever met. This story was too big to not have eyes on it, and he was sure the intelligence officer would try to cover it up. John wasn't sure how he would break the story, but he knew he needed to document it in order to figure that out. They wouldn't give him the helmet footage, and it was more difficult to confiscate his camera's recording.

The hallway passed quickly as they moved at what John could only describe as a trot. Once out onto the tarmac, he could see the lander, and remembered to turn on his own recorder. The team never stopped, moving right past the ground crew and up the lander's ramp.

John allowed himself to breathe easier once the ramp closed, and the lander took off. Colonel Sheikh couldn't do much if he found out at this point, time was important, and he doubted the team would turn around just to kick him out. Most of them anyway; he wasn't totally sure about a couple of them.

As he contemplated, he looked up and over at Granberg. The man hardly ever spoke, mostly just grunted and growled at people. The four words in the briefing room, were the most he had heard the man say at once. He made a point not to stare too long, the man already had his axe out and was working the edge again.

"Any sharper and he'll split an atom," John commented to himself.

Andrews nudged him, "I'm here to protect you from the bad guys, not Granberg dude. Try not to annoy him."

"Why do you think I keep losing at cards?"

Andrews laughed and slapped a hand on his shoulder. John settled into the seat of the lander, and shook his head. The colonial ship was no better than the one from the Australia he had first ridden on. He shifted his weight some until he found a comfortable position.

"Newsie."

John looked up and saw Stewart handing him a small data tablet. It wasn't much larger than the unit on his left forearm for his drone. He rolled it over in his hands and thumbed it on, discovering a list of the team members. Clicking on one, he noticed it brought up a small medical looking file.

"What's this?"

"Redundancy," Stewart said. "Anything gets us separated, you will at least have that information to give whoever is patching who up."

John nodded, suddenly sensing the weight of the object handed to him. He stared at the small device for a long time before latching it onto the harness on his other forearm. He gave Stewart a thumbs up, who nodded to him before leaning back against the bulkhead.

His HUD displayed a line-to-line communication, as he looked at it, the line connected with a beep.

"Newsie," Keith said, "do me a favor and keep your head down during this. These guys aren't to be played with."

"I know the risks, Keith," he replied, "just like before, just like back in Africa. This is my job, I'm no less committed than you."

"That's the part that worries me. You stay glued to Andrews and Stewart. I don't care how tempting the shot might be."

"What drives you to do this?"

"What? Keeping you alive?"

John shook his head, "No, to serve. Going into this situation, like all the others you've been in."

The line was silent for a time, but not closed. John held his breath, wondering if he might have touched a nerve asking Keith that question. He figured if anyone could articulate an answer beyond service, Keith would give him something.

"There are only so many people who can do what we do," Keith said. "That makes it our duty to hold that line."

10

Eversley had slept most of the trip out to the station, waking only when Keith kicked his boot. He sat up and stretched before standing and twisting a few times. Once he settled back into his seat, Keith looked at him, and all he could do was shrug.

"Alright," Keith said, "now that everyone's ready, one last time."

An icon appeared near the station representing the lander, a dotted line moved from it to the station proper. It was adjacent to the hangar bay, showing an external work access hatch. There was a circle around it now, with a red and blue line entering and separating, showing the paths each team would take.

"First squad will secure the hangar area and advance down the cargo halls. Second, will move into the superstructure and make their way to this point," Keith explained, pointing to an area above the promenade and the central tower.

Eversley looked over to Holte and caught her eye long enough to exchange a nod. They had planned to be the team moving through the superstructure. There was no life support in those areas, no air pressure, and almost never any gravity. That made it dangerous, but to his mind, that was half the fun.

The brief went on, going over all the small intricate details they had developed a few hours earlier. Such was the way of being an operator, the detail work was necessary, but very redundant. He had accepted this fact of the universe, so he found the fun where he could.

The minor space infiltration was by far the best part of the operation,; the last moments of peace before the shooting started. Gamma was seldom called up for simple nonviolent operations, this one was different though. Shezlan soldiers were clearly present amid the militants, and that raised so many questions.

Eversley brought himself back to the present as Keith marked the various checkpoints and asked if anyone had anything to add. He wasn't surprised when no one said anything, they had all sat together and built the plan earlier that day. Every operation was a group effort, and by the end, everyone had it committed to memory.

"So," he said, "I'm gonna say it, who thinks this is an invasion?"

Qureshi nodded, "I believe he has a point. Fully armored, and obviously armed Shezlan soldiers involved in an attempted coup?"

"There is no definitive line on this," Keith said, "so the standing order is to treat them as pirates, or at best, hired guns."

"So, no prisoners?" Bekele asked.

Keith shook his head and Eversley sat back, thinking about that. They hadn't been on a kill mission in a long time, and this rescue suddenly turned into one. *Well, that wasn't entirely accurate,* he thought; they knew it the moment they saw the footage.

"What's wrong my friend?" Qureshi asked.

"Nothing, just trying to get into the right headspace," he said.

She smirked at him, "I believe the term you use is, 'bullshit' isn't it?"

Eversley chuckled, few people could call him out, and she was firmly on the list. They had been serving on Gamma the same amount of time. That much time together in the field, training together, built bonds, and some were tighter than others. While close to all the team, he figured about four of them were closer than the others. That meant they knew when someone wasn't being honest.

"Well yeah," he said, "in this instance it's true, just a bit more real than normal, I suppose."

"How so?"

"It's always rough having to kill our own to keep humanity together. Shouldn't it be easier to kill aliens to do the same job?"

Qureshi shrugged, "Perhaps we have taken on that evil, and are not sure how to do a different sort?"

"Killing is killing Q."

"Is it?" She asked, "We take life to protect the larger good of our people, but it is still our own we cull. Now, the Shezlan are killing our fellow humans. We are not taking the lives of detractors to the idea of humanity, but direct foes to it. There is a protective, and justified, thrill mixed with the taking of life."

"I don't follow."

"We feel sorrow for killing misguided of our own. The Shezlan get no such reaction. They are an enemy with evil intent, and we feel vindication for killing them."

"Well, that was a little dark."

She smiled and inclined her head, then looked at the time of arrival. After a moment, she climbed out of the seat, went to her knees, and began to pray. It astounded Eversley how she managed to always know when, and where to face when doing so.

He took a moment to stretch his legs across some, creating a small barrier to anyone moving around. None of them would intentionally bother her, but accidents happened. A quick look around and he saw the usual activity; Granberg sharpening his axe, Pew-Pew was sorting her field kit one last time, and Keith and Holte were talking.

He noticed Andrews, Bekele and Newsie were chatting among themselves. He almost felt sorry for Newsie, they'd have him scammed out of a fair amount of cash, given the chance. Both were decent card players, though Bekele tended to get drunk if the game took too long. Eversley wondered if Newsie knew that yet.

A quick glance showed Harrison, George, and Turgenev doing much the same, amid themselves. Although it sounded more like setting up to take a count and see who got the best score of the day. He almost got upset with them, but in the end, each of the team found a way to resolve what would be happening, so he trusted Keith's judgment to allow it.

Eversley settled on a quiet prayer of his own. It wasn't as pronounced as Qureshi's traditions, but he fell back on it once in a while, and if anger and righteous fury were going to be unleashed, he figured it couldn't hurt to get things right.

When he opened his eyes again, he noticed Qureshi doing much the same for him as he had her. She smiled down and inclined her head as he settled back against the bulkhead again. It was hardly necessary, as far as he was concerned, it was simply a bowed head. The same way people respected her space to pray, he was less worried about being bumped into.

"I've got your six even in the small things," she said, sitting down.

He smiled and nodded, "Thanks."

"It is about that time."

He nodded again, then let out a long sigh. He looked at her and held his hand up with all five fingers out. When she gave him a strange look, he winked, and started to count down. When the last finger folded into his fist, he mouthed as Keith spoke, right on cue.

"Saddle up!"

He and Qureshi exchanged a chuckle as they stood, got their helmets on, and the last of their equipment shouldered. They had already placed some of the stuff on their armor, but the backpacks that secured larger items and equipment, weren't exactly designed to be sat against.

"What are you laughing about?" Holte asked.

Eversley just shrugged, "Just ready to go."

Keith looked back at him and narrowed his eyes as the helmet went on, "I call B.S."

Eversley laughed again, "Think so?"

"Enough," Jubert called out over the com. "Heads in the game, folks."

The light in the interior changed color to a dim red as everyone lined up and did one last seal check on their helmets. He felt Qureshi's hands checking his gear as he checked Stewart's who was in front of him. Assuring that things were in order, he turned to Qureshi and made a spinning motion, doing the same to her gear as she was last in line.

"Hey look at Newsie," came Holte's voice on the com, "he finally got it done in under a minute."

Everyone laughed, they might have started to accept him, but he was still going to be the butt of a few jokes. They tended to take turns picking on one another, but Newsie got priority for now. Eversley felt it was good for him, the guy was solid as far as he was concerned, and in the right line of work. He still couldn't really understand who would willingly go into a firefight unarmed, that was a crazy, even he didn't touch.

The light flashed on and off twice. Keith looked back at everyone, then focused on Eversley. He was already checking everyone around him visually and saw everything was in place. Check and double check was the idea. Seeing no issues, he gave a thumbs up.

"Cabin depressurizing!"

The air was slowly removed from the section they were in. Eversley felt the suit compensate for the pressure change, and felt the familiar feeling of isolation. Even though his team were all standing right there, they still felt distant, as if across a void.

"Approaching drop point; opening hatch."

The door behind him opened, and everyone turned around to face it. *He and Qureshi would be first-in this time.* He smiled at the thought, stepping back to the ramp, feeling everyone else moving behind and beside him. The open void of space stretched out before him; stars as distant points, Tronis and its moons off in the distance, looking about the size of baseballs.

"Good luck," Jubert said over the com, "give 'em hell!"

"Oorah!" came the response from everyone.

Eversley felt his heart pounding, the thrill of the jump, and the coming mission, filling his body. 'Living on the edge of the knife,' as he and some others called it. The proverbial blade was out now, and he felt the smile form on his lips, expanding into a grin.

The light turned a pale green and Eversley dove out into the void. It was a tricky way to deploy, in space there was no up or down, not in the natural sense. He had to break his existing movement and change that momentum in the direction he wanted to go. Here, it was towards the station that was just coming into view.

The combination of the transport's momentum, his suit's thrusters, and his orientation, gave the impression he was skydiving towards the surface. The distance allowed him to see the station's rotation as they approached. His suit's heads up display making the projected path to the target landing site; they were right on course.

"Deceleration," he called out, "orient in five...Four...Three...Two...One!"

At the last count, he activated the various microbursts to orient himself for a landing. His stomach felt cold as his body adjusted to the movement, then started to decelerate. He always found it strange that the human body still managed to maintain a feeling of equilibrium, even in zero gravity.

He bent his knees and waited for the impact, the last few feet to the surface closing in. A few seconds later, one longer microburst, and he felt his feet make contact, touching down like a feather, on the surface of the station. Automated programs kicked in and his boots used a magnetic field to hold him against the station. The only feeling he noticed was the slight lurch in his body as he was now moving the same direction the station was rotating.

"Good touchdown," he called.

The rest of the team settled in behind him at five-foot intervals, each touching as gracefully as he did, coming to rest as their momentum matched their new position. He counted each pair as they settled in, then watched Newsie almost stumble in his landing.

"Did ya puke Newsie?" He asked over the com.

His response was a middle finger salute and a headshake. Eversley chuckled again, wondering if they'd make an operator out of the man yet. He turned towards his destination. *Now, it was time to get to work.*

11

After what seemed like ages, John felt his stomach stop doing loops. The disorientation, and constant change in orientation was far more than he had expected. He did manage not to puke, and was proud of that, almost as much as he was relieved. Between the team's relentless torment, and the foul smell in the visor, he wasn't sure what would have been worse.

After a moment to orient himself, he could see the hatch they planned on using to enter the station. The team moved that direction, and he felt the hand of his handler on his shoulder for the trip. He looked over and saw it was Harrison instead of Andrews, which surprised him as much as anything else.

"Don't worry, Newsie, I'm almost as good at babysitting as Andrews is."

John shook his head, and they moved with the team, "How'd you get stuck on my detail?"

"Lost a bet."

"Seriously?"

Harrison nodded, "Yep, Andrews called a marker in from a previous bet we made about Eversley and Granberg."

"You bet wrong, eh?"

"It was an eating contest! Could have gone either way honestly. Who knew Granberg could eat that many hot wings without a beer?"

John laughed, he knew there was plenty of gambling going on, but he wasn't sure exactly how it overrode Keith or Jubert's word; not that they had told him who was going to be watching him. He figured it was a standing assignment, evidently, that wasn't the case.

"I'll get you through it," Harrison said.

"I know," John replied, "be too much bad PR."

John got his helmet camera going and set up his drone. It couldn't fly now, but it would be helpful once they got inside. For now, he watched his footage to see where he was in orientation to things. Even though he had a different escort, he was still in the same place, parked right behind Stewart, which made sense given the amount of medical gear he was carrying.

"Everybody hold here," Qureshi said, via the com.

The team shuffled, crouched, and kneeled, looking outwards over the smooth surface of the station. There was nothing for anyone to hide behind, but that also meant there was no cover behind. John felt the idea of a fight out on the surface to be insane, but insane was common for Gamma.

"There's an entry denial device here," Eversley said.

John looked and zoomed his camera in more, watching Eversley and Qureshi examine the hatch carefully. Eversley had one of his combat suits' cord cameras out and was fishing it into the station somehow; Qureshi was doing something similar with hers.

"Eversley, freeze," Qureshi said.

John felt his blood run cold at the tone in her voice. The feeling was magnified by just how quickly Eversley did as she said; the man was practically a statue in the blink of an eye.

"Device," she said, "just next to where your camera was moving. Come my direction with it, half an inch, then up and out."

After Eversley did as she told him, he moved away carefully, then she retracted her camera and moved back as well. Both of them looked back at the team and exchanged a quick fist bump.

"Pew-Pew," Keith said, "get to work."

John watched Silverling move out of the formation and start sorting through her pack as she moved up. He had to remind himself not to say anything, he almost opposed the very idea. Then his senses got ahold of him; this was what she did, and was good at.

"Tell me what you saw," she said to Qureshi.

As the two went to a direct line, John was unable to listen beyond that point. Keith was on the team's line, however. He had already informed Jubert of what was happening and said something about pivoting.

"Alright everyone," Keith said, "depending on how this goes, we might be hunting a different entry point."

"We could cut into the panels, a safe distance from the hatch," Granberg said, "just open space under most of this isn't it?"

"Yes, but that'd set off the structural alarm for a breach. Be the same as just flying a shuttle into the hangar."

John looked at his direct link and looked at Harrison, "Huh?"

"Safety system, if there is any sort of penetrating impact on the station exterior, it would alert the sensors that there was a hole someplace there wasn't supposed to be; the hatches even have an indicator of being opened properly or not," Harrison explained.

"Oh, so that means no blasting through the door."

Harrison nodded, and John went back to listening to the overall conversation.

"Let's assume all the hatches have some similar set up," Andrews said, "there is an umbilical about five hundred meters away from the hangar."

"That's kind of an obvious entry," Bekele said.

"They can't lock the whole place down," Andrews said, "with what? A few dozen? A hundred? This place would need a regiment to properly lock down."

John focused on what Silverling was doing, zooming his camera back in, and watching patiently. She had her pack out, some cords and her various tools just floating freely around her. She kept them sorted out like she had a wall mounted storage bracket in normal gravity.

There was a camera cord pushed into the space Eversley's had previously occupied; another cable in it as well, one he thought was likely a cutting tool. *It could just be a different sort of camera.* He wasn't about to bother her in the midst of her project, that would be a quick way to end up floating back to Tronis.

"If we select an alternate entry," Keith said, "the first thing to keep in mind is, they'll know, and this mission will go loud much sooner than planned."

John heard Granberg's growl over the line, he wasn't sure if the man sounded eager or just crazy. The time he had spent doing stories around the military meant he knew some of the insider language. The phrase they were tossing around, 'going loud', meant the shooting would be intense and violent. The quiet and careful operation would be over, then it would be a fight to the finish, he wasn't sure he was ready to have a front-row seat for that show.

"Hey Keith," Silverling said, "I don't think we have to worry about going loud. I've got a small counter charge set up on the device. We can open the door after it's cleared."

John blinked, he wasn't sure how long she had been working on it. She had told him she was good at what she did, while he didn't doubt her, he knew it for a fact now. The other option was, the person who put it there was inept, but he let that thought run off and hide where it should.

Silverling cleaned up her work and started to move away from the hatch while extending a cord from the wrist of her armor. Once she was near everyone else, she looked around and held up three fingers. John was sure he saw a smile on her face through the visor, as she started the rapid countdown to zero.

It was surreal, the flash and the minor almost imperceptible thump in his feet, in total silence. He wondered if it was his mind putting in the bass sound; he was sure he could have heard. Sound didn't travel in space, so he shouldn't have heard the blast, regardless of how large it was.

"Gods," Holte said, "you scare me sometimes Pew-Pew."

Everyone chuckled, and John once again wondered if he wasn't insane for wanting to film them. Though it was a great insight into their dynamics, to the point he planned on making commentary about it; especially in this instance.

"Alright," Keith said, "time to get to work. Eversley, Qureshi, you're up again."

John watched them both move to the hatch again, poking and prodding the damaged door to peel it open. He wasn't sure exactly what was happening at first, then after a bit of thought

John recalled, they were originally disabling the sensor on the door. Eversley gave everyone a thumbs up, then vanished into the hole.

John was holding his breath, waiting to know that things were alright. He watched the others, but couldn't get a good read out of their body language. He figured after a bit more time he'd be able to, but for now, he presumed the stress was irrelevant to them.

"We are clear," Qureshi said.

"Good copy," replied Keith, "alright Gamma, let's get to work."

With his words, the team moved forward carefully but quickly. John quickly set his camera back to its normal setting; he didn't want to lose any good footage due to being zoomed clear in on an elbow or backpack.

John took a moment to take a breath before jumping into the hatch, falling slowly into the superstructure of the station. John estimated he was just five feet away from the hatch when Stewart reached out his hand and pulled him onto the walkway, which would typically extend to the hatch, when opened.

When he looked down, the lack of open space surprised him. He expected it to be a large open area, and was not planning to see all the walkways, frames, and supports. John looked back and offered to help Harrison over as he descended in.

"Thanks," Harrison said.

"Everyone in?" Keith asked.

No one answered while the chain of bodies moved along the narrow walkway. John wasn't as steady in minimal gravity as the rest of them were, but he made sure not to slow them down. Having Harrison pushing, and Stewart dragging him, left little choice in the matter.

It took a moment to realize he needed to use the heads-up display's enhanced imager. Once it was up, he could see how much space there was between the various stations. There was still far less open area than he expected, but more than he thought after entry.

It only took a few minutes for the team to get to the separation point. He watched Keith and Holte exchange a fist bump, while the teams flowed in their different directions. John felt himself swept up with Keith's team, and after a quick glance at Harrison, he just accepted the fact.

John watched forward again as they made their way to the hangar. There were only a couple of changes in direction between their entry, and the access air lock to the hangar section. He allowed himself a moment's pride because he could recall the layout they had shown him, and was keeping a decent account of their location mentally.

After the second turn, Keith held his hand up and John watched everyone freeze. John knelt with Harrison and Stewart, looking around to see if there was some sort of threat. There was nothing to be seen. John was about to ask what was happening when he heard Keith on the radio,

"First squad to Overwatch," Keith said. "We've reach entry point and are holding."

Jubert's voice came over the line, "Good copy, have you holding at entry point. Be advised, we still do not have access to internal sensors. Advise that you hold until we gain access to network."

"Copy that," Keith said "Alright everyone, looks like we get comfy for a bit."

John settled in, much like the rest of the team, resting on his heels. It hadn't taken him long to appreciate the minor tricks they had shown him. Squatting down as he was and settling his weight felt good after the space drop, and the walk through the station to this point. He had expected zero atmosphere and minimal gravity to be easier to move in.

12

Eversley moved cautiously along the various girders of the station. Since the walkway no longer allowed his team access to the section they needed, Eversley was forced to navigate the superstructure. He didn't mind it, in any other situation he might have found it fun, but for now he would settle for it not being bothersome.

Each support and junction of cables offered another chance to find what he needed. If he could find the one box that had the station's monitoring system, the team would be able to fully coordinate and take away the advantage. He held no delusions, the people who were here had helped build the place and knew it better than the back of their hands.

The station plans only showed so much, mostly how the place *should* look when finished. While it was close to being done, Eversley wasn't stupid enough to think the people on the station hadn't adjusted the plans, knowing they'd be doing this. He was especially certain they planned on the people being sent to stop them having access to the plans, and therefore able to plan an attack.

"How's it coming up there two-two?" Holte asked via the com.

"Not great," he said. "I've passed six junctions and not one had access to what we need."

"Alright, keep it short, we can look other places too."

Eversley nodded to himself, making his way to the next box he could see. It was tedious work, even with enjoying the problem solving and crawling around the supports. He was getting a decent workout mentally and physically on this mission. The idea that they may have specifically not installed a unit in the outer section did cross his mind, and if it weren't for the booby trap at the door, he'd have already given up.

"They knew it was a vulnerability," he told himself. "That means there is more than just the way in we took."

Once he reached the junction box, he pulled his knife back out, sliding the edge between the security tie and the box. A flick of his wrist and the sharp edge went right through the bright red plastic. He opened the box and almost cheered; the right cables were being shunted through the box, along with dozens of others.

"Two-two for two-one," he said, "got it!"

"Excellent," Holte said.

Eversley pulled out the link cords from his suit, attaching them to various ports. Once hooked up, he took a small device and moved it over each line. It allowed a brief local connection so he could see what each one was. It took only two tries, and he had the right line; the data coming into his HUD was the station's status network.

"Attaching the hijacker to the line," he said aloud.

There was a pair of beeps and then a vibration in his forearm as the suit's wrist device came to life. He glanced down and saw the data for the station coming on the screen. There was the menu screen, all the options, and the status of the various sensors around the station.

"Two-two for Two-one," he said, "we're in."

The path back was less problematic, as he didn't need to investigate each junction box he passed. He could release the magnetics of his boots to allow him to move in the minimalistic gravity more freely. The process was like swinging on monkey bars as a kid, except without the falling to the ground bit.

Once he crossed onto the catwalk support rail, he gave Holte a thumbs up and readjusted his equipment. He wanted his rifle back in hand, and to be back on point. Floating through the station meant all his gear had to be stowed, and that made him feel vulnerable.

"Overwatch to all," came Jubert's voice, "accessing the network. Going to maintain a low profile, so I'll only switch off sensors you are about to deal with."

"Copy that," said Holte, "Eversley, back on point. Saddle up everyone."

Eversley felt the grin spread on his face as he made his way to position. He glanced back long enough to get a thumbs up from Holte and was off. The next area they needed to get to would allow them to access the station quietly, and with any luck, be in the general vicinity to the Colonial Director.

He made the next two turns on the walkway, came to a hatch, then looked at his HUD and double checked the serial number. They matched. He let out a breath, the airlock was not huge, but was large enough so the squad could all get in. He figured they designed it for workers to go on shift, or to move equipment in and out with some sort of efficiency.

"Two-two for Two-one," he said, "got the hatch, door is green."

Holte's voice came back, "Good copy, moving up to you. Two-one for Overwatch. We are at check point Hudson."

"Copy, first squad just passed Ark. Coordinated entry on your go."

"Copy," Holte said, looking at Eversley, "do it."

Eversley watched the hatch's green light blink off and spun the access wheel. There was no outrush of air or debris, and a quick glance showed the darkroom to be empty. He raised his weapon and stepped in, moving to the far door with the rest of the squad behind him. Once the door was secure again, he accessed the panel to re-pressurize the room.

"Two-two for all," he said, "making entry."

The door led him into a large room still set up for construction, there was equipment, tools, and spacesuits. The lights were off, but through his HUD, he could make out the details of the room; including the light markers of his teammates' weapons as they panned the room as well. He shifted his attention to the only other door and moved towards it.

A moment later, Holte's hand was on his shoulder, giving him a squeeze. He tapped the keypad, and the door slid open. Eversley panned the door carefully, then moved out into the hallway. Three doors lined the hall, and according to the layout, they were planned to be living quarters for the work crews.

Eversley went to the first door as others moved past him to take positions at the other two. Holte stood across from him and, at a nod, he tapped the door to slide open and moved in quickly. He looked to the corner, then panned to his right as he moved. He could see Holte's gun light moving to converge to his and they crossed. The room was clear, he raised his rifle up to the ceiling and seeing Holte do the same, he moved back to the door.

The rest of the squad came out of their rooms signaling all clear. Eversley moved to the head of the squad and made his way down the rest of the corridor until it opened out to a recreation room. He again panned the door and saw two people at the far side of the room.

Eversley moved back out of their line of sight and signaled Holte. She nodded, and he again panned into the doorway, leveling his rifle at one of the two. Neither was looking towards the door, so he and Holte both took aim, and fired. Both weapons were LSR-10s, high energy laser weapons, that were accurate and most importantly, quiet.

A barely audible sizzle sound was all that anyone could hear as the beam burnt away the various molecules in the air between the emitter and the target. The targets suddenly twitched as a brief pulse of energy burned a hole in their backs and the cabinets in front of them. The beams hitting a person caused a sound that reminded Eversley of an air hose, as it suddenly super-heated the fluids and burned away the tissue. The momentary hiss and thud signaled they had hit their mark.

Eversley moved forward as soon as they hit the ground, with his weapon aimed at the door on the far side of the room. He could feel Holte on his heels, as well as the rest of the squad, filtering into the room. The door slid open, and he carefully panned the space into the hall beyond, offering only his muzzle to any potential threat.

The next hall led to the walkway that went around the promenade, and he could see two doors at the far end. Each had a large picture window looking into the hall, and light pouring from them. The occasional shadow flittered the light.

"I don't imagine this staying quiet much longer," he said to Holte.

"Yeah," she said. "I'm willing to bet these two went for coffee for everyone."

Eversley nodded, half expecting someone to open a door and yell at their friends to hurry up. That would be just what this mission needed, the alert going off before they got control of the walkway. He didn't like the idea of fighting the entire group of station workers with just a team of six, even with heavy weapons in the mix.

Holte was leaning against his shoulder, looking the way he was indicating with his rifle. He felt a tap on his shoulder, and the pressure of her body move back away from him. He waited a second and then moved back into the room as well, closing the door enough to let his camera cord out.

"Thoughts," Holte asked everyone.

"If we push the rooms," Turgenev said in his Slavic tones, "we will be in an open firefight. There is no way around this."

Eversley nodded, "That's our job in this case, but I'd like to buy us time to deal with whoever is in those rooms before everyone starts trying to shoot us."

Holte nodded, "Right, our job will be to provide overhead fire support for First Squad as they push that tower."

"Let's just have Jubes lock the rooms down remotely," Andrews said. "Take them outta the fight."

"No guarantee they don't have the override codes for the safety doors," countered Bekele.

Eversley nodded again, glancing at the screen on his HUD showing the doors. He really didn't want them to come out and ambush the team amid planning. There would be a list of people giving them hell for the rest of their lives over that kind of stunt.

"We can't hold long," Holte said, "this situation is going loud whether we like it or not."

Eversley recovered his camera cord and moved to cover the end of the hall with his rifle again. He saw no sense in beating around the bush, they'd decide how to breach and that would be it. The best plan he had was a couple of swarmer grenades, breach and clear in one package.

"Two-one for all elements," Holte said on the com, "calling an audible."

"One-one for Two-one," came Keith's voice, "what'd ya have in mind?"

Eversley listened as Holte laid out her plan and smiled. He and the others would push up on the rooms and blast them both with swarmers. Once they cleared them, they would use the rooms as cover to clear any supporting enemies off the walkways and sky bridge above the promenade. Keith and his team would clear out all the ones who made the mistake of looking up at the fire fight.

"Alright," Holte said, "on you Eversley."

He surged forward, a smooth, deliberate pace taking him the short distance down the hall. He crouched and moved low under the window as the others did the same. He, Holte, and Bekele were under the right-side window, while the others were under the left. Thumbs up were exchanged all around as everyone sat into position, then Holte and Andrews pulled out their swarmers.

"On three," Holte said, "two...One...Execute!"

13

John knew the explosion was coming, he distinctly remembered the conversation. He was positive he wouldn't jump; it was so far away, and he knew it was coming. There was absolutely no possible way he was going to flinch, jump, or yelp. That was his plan at least, and to quote many on the team, '*Best laid plans don't always get one laid the way one plans.*'

He wasn't sure what was worse, the act of doing so, or the fact that no one noticed. That they might have gotten used to his inexperience, or the fact he wasn't as hardened as he thought he should be. The latter might have hurt less than he thought initially.

Harrison wasn't hanging on to his shoulder, but John could feel the man's knee pressed on his leg. John wanted to twist out from under him, but thought better as Harrison was aiming. The shooting was going to start, and John knew better than to mess with that. Instead, he cued his camera drone up and panned the area the battle would be occurring in.

The silence was almost maddening. No one spoke, only body motions as the team took aim from the shadows of the hallway. Then people stood, aimed their weapons upwards toward the explosion, and now relentless weapon fire. First Squad started to shoot them down with a ruthless efficiency that terrified John.

He looked up at Harrison, who was firing his rifle in single shot mode. A single loud crack, a slight shift in his orientation, followed by another crack. John looked at the camera feed from the drone and watched a man in orange overalls drop to the floor, a rifle clattering away. The first person to move towards the man dropped in the same instant as a crack from Harrison's rifle.

Keith's voice came over the com in his helmet, "All elements, move up."

John panned the drone back to the hallway, getting what he felt was a spectacular aerial view of the team coming out into the promenade, weapons out and firing as they moved to the first barricades. The station workers had set up several defensible positions, and as typical, Gamma was using the tools of the enemy against them.

First Squad moved with a fierce aggression; going from one position to the next. Each time they moved he noticed more and more people in orange suits on the floor. John watched through the feed with a chill he couldn't understand; something about the scene seemed wrong to him.

He felt himself shudder as he watched Silverling point her weapon at someone on the floor and fire. Soon as she did, without a second glance, she moved towards another who was shooting at her from a different barricade. His heart felt like it was in his throat as he saw the rifle fire at her, and clearly, hit its mark.

"Breathe, man," Harrison said, "that stuff is rated to take hits up to five thousand feet per second."

John looked up at him, "Huh?"

"The body armor you dunce," Harrison said. "It'll take a rifle the caliber of mine to get through it."

John nodded and let out a breath he didn't notice he had been holding. Harrison seemed to notice he was sitting on him and moved. John wasted no time in getting his feet under him and activated his helmet's camera. He made sure to get the up-close footage of Harrison as he put his weapon to use.

Once he was satisfied with that, he moved his head around the barricade to get a better view. The angle was awkward, but he was getting some interesting shots as one or another of the team would filter through his field of view. Then, he saw Granberg and one worker get into a close fight. The worker had jumped out from some hidden space and now had their hands on Granberg's rifle.

The man was larger than Granberg by easily a hundred pounds. Unsurprisingly, it did him no good. John watched as Granberg twisted and punched the man in the face, then reached for the axe on his belt. The morbid horror John felt seep into his stomach was an unfamiliar sensation. He was transfixed on the micro fight within the larger battle.

Granberg chopped downwards into the man's knee, then in the same motion, withdrew it, and changed his grip. He had the axe just below the head, all but ignoring the handle, as he punched repeatedly into the side of his attacker. His thumb at the top, holding the axe in position, as he used it like some sort of extension of his fist.

The man stumbled back away, holding up a hand, only to have it batted away by Granberg's off-hand. His grip on the axe changed again, now at the base of the handle, swinging it more like a club. The back blunt side of the axe head struck the man in the face, sending blood and gore away onto the barricade next to the two combatants.

John rolled away, unable to continue watching, as the faceplate on his helmet reflexively retracted. His head was spinning, and he had to focus on his breathing for a moment.

The thundering of his heart was in his ears as well, drowning out whatever was being said to him by Harrison. He really didn't care to hear the man's joke at the moment.

"Newsie," Harrison yelled again.

John shook his head and looked back at the man, "Yeah, I'm here."

Harrison grinned, "Good. Still didn't puke I see."

"Not for lack of wanting to."

John breathed a sigh of relief as Harrison went back to shooting. The callous way Harrison was about the surrounding death bordered on sickening. He had been in the field before, but he was certainly seeing a new side of the team today. John tried to focus on what was so different .*Why was this worse than in the pirate base?*

The idea that Silverling was much the same at the moment was hard to process. She always seemed so kind, easygoing, and gentle. John admitted to himself it was a strange balance. She was an operator in a special forces team, so she was clearly capable of violence. He decided it was the coldness that bothered him, the ease with which taking a life seemed to roll off of them.

As John considered the implications, something, in the shadows down the hall they came from, drew his eyes off the feed from the drone. It wasn't anything he could say he saw, more a sense that the darkness down the unused corridor moved. Then, a plasma round struck the barricade he and Harrison were hiding behind. It reflected the flash from the far side, for just a moment, on visors.

"Harrison!"

John tried to scramble to his feet, then suddenly felt himself being lifted and thrown in front of the barricade. He hit the ground with a grunt and again tried to get his feet under him. He frantically looked to see what sort of danger was on this new side, but was relieved to see none of the workers there waiting with a gun.

"Contact six," Harrison was shouting into the com as he dove over, "multiple hostiles from our entry point."

"They have armor on," John said.

"Yep," he replied, "and they are packing heavy firepower."

"Those aren't station workers with guns."

"Nope," Harrison grumbled as he hunkered down.

John felt thumps against the barricade. He imagined the weapons being used, striking the space he and Harrison had just occupied. *A moment or two more.* If he hadn't seen something, they both would have been in serious danger.

"Who are they?"

Harrison chuckled, "My bet is the Shezlan we saw in the feed."

"Oh God." John felt a chill and a pit in his stomach.

"One-six for one-one," Harrison said over the com, "we are taking fire from the entry point, heavily armed and armored, likely Shezlan."

"Copy," Keith answered calmly. "One-two, One-five, fall back to One-six and provide support. Keep them out of the promenade."

John went back to the drone's view and watched Granberg and Silverling disengage from the battles they were in. Each moved in tandem with the other, getting closer to one another as they closed the distance to get to him and Harrison. They both fired bursts of ballistic fire as they came, and John was sure the Shezlan were regretting their choice to engage Gamma.

Keith's voice came over the com in an angry bark, "Newsie, you hearing me?"

"Huh? Yeah, I hear you," John replied.

"Move your ass and get up to One-three. Now!"

John slipped past Silverling and Granberg as nimbly as possible, making for the next bit of cover. He remembered one thing he'd been told early in his career when covering war zones. He had to keep himself below the line of cover, his head had to stay below the barricades. He scrambled on all fours, following the indicator on his HUD guiding him to Stewart.

He leaned against the third barricade, panting for breath. John looked to his left and instantly regretted it, his eyes landing on the corpse of a worker still holding a rifle. The lifeless eyes of the man staring back at him caused him to shudder. He also felt he had rested enough and made to move again.

He hadn't gone far when he felt himself get lifted, the side of Quereshi's laser rifle filling his peripheral. John stumbled forward, using his arms to balance more than anything else, as they rounded a barricade. He felt her shove him forward, to the ground, at Stewart's feet.

"I found something of yours," she said.

John rolled onto his back and swallowed the indignant feeling that almost tainted his choice of words. Stewart had barely glanced down, then was back to firing his laser at someone John couldn't see. He managed to get into a sitting position and squeezed between the two operators as they went about their deadly business.

"I'm not sure what Allah has in mind for you," Qureshi said, "but he clearly had a hand on you during that run."

"What are you talking about?"

"Half these idiots thought you looked like a good target!"

"If you say so."

John looked back at the drone feed and wished he hadn't. The screen had dozens of red squares indicating attacking hostile units. He glanced at the controls, saw they had overridden him, and realized a new user had control. More of the functions were open and being utilized; something they did not give him access to. *For obvious reasons.*

Keith's voice was in his ear again, "One-one for Two-one, where is my fire support?"

"We're working on it," Holte snapped back. "Someone thought it'd be fun to invite the Shezlan to the party."

"I noticed. How's it looking up there?"

"Tense."

"Can you hold?"

"Yeah," Holte was panting. "Let me sort this out and you'll have overhead fire."

John felt his throat go dry, the sound in her voice was unlike anything he had heard before. His experiences with Holte were better than with most of the team, and he had never heard fear in her voice. He wasn't sure if that was what he heard, but it certainly wasn't her usual confidence.

"Two-two for all of First Squad," came Eversley's voice, "get small! Swarmers inbound from above."

John was instantly smothered by Stewart and Qureshi's bodies as they pressed tightly into the cover. He wasn't sure if it was just for cover or their inclination to protect him. At that moment, he wasn't sure it mattered. He had seen swarmers' effects once before, only the aftermath. Now, he was in the line of fire.

He noticed it wasn't just one, but four different explosions. He felt the flooring rumble underneath him, even the barricade shook, as the shockwave spread over the battlefield. He could see the drone feed, the blasts occurred all around the icons indicating him and the others. He saw people flung and others ran, diving for cover. Just as he started to breathe a sigh of relief, the workers who had been shooting started to get up, and there were suddenly dozens of smaller explosions.

14

Eversley vaulted back behind the wall as ballistic rounds and plasma peppered it. He smiled over at Holte and shrugged. He knew she was likely thinking of some extra words to put in his file, but that was a tomorrow problem. They had to get through today for it to matter.

"What the fuck is the matter with you?" Holte snapped.

Eversley chuckled, "You want that list itemized?"

"Whatever," she said. "Alright second, listen up. We need to clear out these fire teams. First is needing cover fire from on high."

Eversley moved to fire again on the group that was keeping their heads down. The sizzling pop of the laser burning the molecules between him and his target was quiet, and not as imposing as the automatic weapons. It did however, have the desired effect when the laser burnt through their cover and took one down.

He had to duck back down as the enemy's weapons fire slammed into his cover. The one issue he had with the LSR was its slower rate of fire. As far as stopping power and penetration, it was unmatched; just–slow. While he could shoot through most cover, he needed the time to shoot, and dodging the heavy fire complicated that.

Holte shouted, "Bekele, put that coil gun on the group at three o'clock. Turgenev put yours on the ones at nine o'clock. Eversley and George, trade out and get on rear guard."

Eversley moved, staying low as he went, and tapped the large, East African man on the shoulder to tell him he was 'good to go'. He always marveled at Bekele's solidness, though he attributed more credit to the weapon system he used, rather than a workout program. He tried out for a coil gun team once, the weight of the weapon felt ridiculous.

Once George was on the other side, he gave the man a quick fist bump, and they both eyed the corridor they had entered from. He was sure based on the layout that they cleared the only space that allowed access there, but with the Shezlan being involved in the fight, there was no sense in taking a chance.

Eversley listened as Holte directed Andrews to join her in picking off the enemy shooters. He spared a glance back for just a moment, watching the pair set up where he had been, alternating their fire at the different positions. The high-pitched whirling sound that preceded the sonic booms of the coil rounds reached his ears and he grinned.

"Send the rain boys," he said to himself as he looked back down the corridor.

"Movement at the break room door," George said.

Eversley brought his full attention back to the hall, putting his target reticle on the door frame. The moment he saw a target, he planned on sending them into the next life. A quick prayer of his own and he started applying the slightest pressure to his trigger until he felt the tension that told him it was a hair from firing.

"How did they get in there?" George asked.

"They know the station. Either an access hatch that's not marked, or they cut their way in from somewhere else," Eversley replied.

Eversley noticed a flicker in the light above him, nothing he could say was perceptible, but the lights seemed to dim, ever so slightly, for a moment. He spared a glance up, cautious to take his eyes off the door, but not wanting to ignore anything on the battlefield.

He noticed the light flicker again, this time more noticeably even George glanced up. Eversley felt the hairs on the back of his neck stand up, and he knew something was about to happen. He moved his muzzle from the door to the ceiling near the light.

"Two-two for Two-one," he said into the com, "we are about to take contact. Unknown enemy appears to be preparing a breach. I'm going to pop some shots."

"Good copy," Holte replied.

"Time to stir up the shit," he said to George. "Watch that door."

Once the nod came, Eversley looked back to the light and panned his muzzle. He was imagining himself, trying to breach from the ceiling. *What would his approach be? How would he move?* Finally settling on an idea, he aimed, squeezed his trigger past its break, and set off the laser.

The familiar burnt smell, and the emitter hum, filled the air as sparks, then a hole appeared next to the light. He could hear the shout of pain, and it wasn't human. He panned and fired again; this time, into the ceiling closer to his position.

George's rifle suddenly erupted next to him as he started sending bursts of fire at the door that had slid open unexpectedly. Eversley panned his muzzle back in line with the door just in time to see a heavily armored-Shezlan soldier coming through, firing as they came. He didn't give them a chance to get him sighted in, as he squeezed the trigger again.

"Contact six!"

Eversley sent shot after shot into the space of the door as other Shezlan tried to pull their comrade clear of the line of fire. He wasn't completely sure where people were past the door, but he knew they'd be there pulling the downed shooter out of the way, or trying to provide covering fire. The next thing to come out of the room was a grenade, bouncing off the wall and angling back towards him and George.

"Cover!" Eversley shouted to George.

Both men moved back behind the corners as shrapnel flew outwards, slicing through anything in its path. The concussive wave rattled his ears, but being out of the hall, it didn't affect him or George. He brought his muzzle around the corner and caught the next Shezlan moving through the door in the chest.

Plasma and kinetic rounds poured out as they fell, forcing him and George back into cover once more. The bullets punched through the metal frame and housing. Eversley had to duck down lower before panning and firing again.

"Two-One for Two-two," Holte called out, "you hold that position. They get out and we are all in serious trouble."

"No kidding," Eversley snapped back.

"Do something about it!"

Eversley grumbled to himself and looked back over to George who was firing full auto into the hall. He spotted two grenades still on the man's belt and grinned. If they could bounce and deflect it down a hall, so could he.

"George," he called.

The man kept firing, not acknowledging his call. Eversley looked around and found a piece of debris on the floor. A quick chuck and it bounded off the man's side. When he looked over, Eversley made a motion to his belt.

"Huh?"

Eversley swore, "Dude, gimme your grenades!"

He fired again at the door and motioned for Eversley to take over. As he sent more laser bursts down the hall, he felt the grenade pouch thump on the floor by his knee. Once George took over firing on the door, he scooped them up and checked what was there. He had already collected everyone's swarmer grenades, so all that was left were the basic fragmentation ones.

Eversley set them out against his knee and then glanced at the hall. George had injured another and was keeping their help at bay. He took a moment and then found a spot that he figured would get his grenade in the doorway. He took a deep breath and pulled the pin, keeping the spoon locked in place with his hand.

"On two, bud," he called over to George.

After getting a thumbs up he started counting, one, two, and then just as George started to fire again, he threw. The grenade sailed through the air, hit the section of the wall he wanted, and bounced through the opening. The explosion occurred just a moment later, the sound of shrapnel peppering walls, along with shouts of the enemy, told him he hit the mark.

Just to be sure, he sent a second one the same way. When it went off the screams stopped, and there were no other sounds. Eversley took a moment and let out a breath as he motioned for George to cover him. He got up and slipped out of the doorway with his rifle leveled at the corner of the door.

He stopped at the corner, took one last deep breath, then moved around the corner and peered into the room. There was no movement, just five human bodies, along with five Shezlan.

He turned back to give George a thumbs up when he saw sparks and a blast from the ceiling above him.

A pair of Shezlan dropped from the ceiling and started firing. George was on the floor, rolling on his back to fire. Eversley fired at the one above him with the laser set to full, it would drain the battery, but it would burn through Shezlan body armor. The shot connected, and it dropped just as it aimed at George.

George fired at the other one, and Eversley saw at least three of the rounds penetrated. He could see the red blood pouring from the wounds. He started to swap out the battery when the Shezlan reached down, grabbed George by his vest, and hoisted the man off the ground, throwing him over the rail.

Eversley shot the alien repeatedly, as fast as the rifle could. Advancing towards it as he fired, forgetting the weapon was set to full, he only got six shots. Each shot pierced the armor, and the body protected underneath it.

"Two-two for One-one," Eversley shouted, "George just got tossed over the rail at you guys!"

"One-one copies," came Keith's voice, "we got him man. Mind on mission."

"What the hell is going on over there?" demanded Holte.

"Six is secure," Eversley said, "but one tossed George down to the promenade."

"Copy, move to support Bekele, we've got more Shezlan."

He wanted to run to the rail and check on George, but he was still in a fight. Eversley grabbed Geroge's rifle and moved to where Bekele was. Tapping the man on the shoulder, he moved into position with him.

"How we looking?"

"Shit," Bekele said in his drawn-out accent, "they aren't dying quick enough."

"Well, let's fix that," Eversley said and opened up on the covered position with his laser rifle.

The coil gun had already perforated the space, and it did not hinder the laser either. Each shot burned through instantly and found targets taking cover with ease. Based on the screams and shouts, Eversley assumed they were unarmored.

"I've got one more grenade," Eversley said as he moved back to cover.

"Send it man," Bekele shouted over the thunder of the coil gun.

Eversley prepped the grenade and readied his throw, "On you."

Bekele fired two more bursts, then stopped firing. Eversley used that as his signal, released the spoon, and tossed the grenade the distance across to the covered position, "Frag out."

Bekele fired again and the thudding sounds of coil gun rounds breaking the sound barrier drowned out any further shouts. When he released the trigger, all Eversley could hear was the whining of the power pack. There was no further return fire from the position, and after a few moments of waiting, he looked back over to Holte's position.

"Looks like we are clear on this side," he said into the com.

"Good copy," Holte said, "looks good here too. Sweep and be sure. Coil guns, get ready to pour down fire support for First Squad."

"Copy."

Eversley moved ahead of Bekele, who gave him a thumbs up, keeping the coil gun pointed at where he was going. He moved around the slight curve of the walkway, approached the doorway, and barricaded the position the enemy had been using. Peering over and sweeping his muzzle right to left, then through the doorway.

It was a small room, likely supposed to be an observation room or small shop upon completion. There were more than a few bodies, unarmored fools as far as Eversley was concerned. If there was ever a better example of the need for armor and tactics, he didn't know it.

"Rooms clear," he said, "nothing but soup in here."

15

John moved, briefly, out from behind the makeshift barricade as Qureshi and Stewart ran to their teammate. Stewart had told him, in no uncertain terms, to stay there unless he called. He said nothing about watching, and the shot was too incredible to pass up. There was also the fact that if he was filming, he felt fearless. His energy was in getting the shot, not worrying about getting shot.

He looked over towards Keith, watching the man fire on the barricades that still protected those fighting the team. John found himself calmed by how easy the man made it look, the fact he wasn't just spraying but methodically shooting and moving to another position. He had no idea what the strategy was about, that would have to wait till after they were home, but it was keeping the bullets and laser blasts away from Qureshi and Stewart.

"Six, how's it looking back there?" Keith's voice was calm as it came over the com line.

John noticed he was holding his breath, waiting to hear Harrison's response. The three of them were in a dangerous situation, holding that position. He felt the fear creep back into him, not even filming could pull that away.

"Could do with some more shooters to be honest," Harrison rasped in reply.

"Good copy," Keith said, "One-three, if you can get free, get over there."

"George is hurt pretty bad, Chief," she replied.

"I know, but we need to win the fight, or it won't matter."

Qureshi's voice sounded hollow to John as she agreed. Moments later, he saw her sprinting her way past, towards the fight. He kept his camera on her until she was past the barricades, and he lost sight. After a last glance back, he looked towards Stewart and while filming, wished he could be more helpful.

"Get small," came Holte's voice, "rain's coming."

John tried to squeeze himself against the barricade he was beside, covering his head, he started to pray. The sonic booms of the coil gun rounds screaming through the air filled his ears as he felt the impact through the floor. It reminded him of being back on Earth, during a hailstorm, or a cloudburst during a thunderstorm.

Less than thirty seconds later, the downpour of ammunition stopped. John poked his head up and looked all around the promenade. It was eerily silent, then he could see Keith moving carefully, shooting at the ground. John realized his suit's helmet had engaged its hearing protection protocols.

He turned the setting off with a glance at his HUD, then he could hear the cries of pain, mixed with the battle happening in the corridor. An involuntary shudder went down his back as a report from Keith's rifle ended one cry of pain. He quickly cued up the drone and breathed a sigh of relief, as it had somehow managed to not be obliterated in the onslaught.

"Newsie," Stewart shouted, "get over here. I need my extra packs."

John looked around and doing his best bear crawl, made his way over to Stewart. He nearly fell on his face when he got there and was unsurprised when Stewart barely paid any mind.

He was already pulling one compartment open to retrieve another medical kit.

"How bad is he?"

Stewart shook his head, "Not good, internal bleeding, broken ribs, arm, leg, you name it."

"Shit," John breathed as he tried to pull some packs free.

"You just give me what I tell you," Stewart directed as he worked.

John noticed that Stewart and Qureshi had done a considerable amount already. George's right leg was wrapped and splinted already. He was on his back and Stewart had already cleared the man's helmet to start putting on a brace.

"He'll need more plasma," Stewart said, pointing to an IV that had already been inserted.

John reached down and snatched one of the bags in the kits he carried. He had to take a deep breath and think back to what Stewart had shown him. After a moment's thought, John turned on the noise filter on his helmet, dialing it to only let him hear the person next to him.

Once that was in order and he could focus, John set the replacement bag next to the one attached to George. He then found the coupler, and took it in both hands, giving a counterclockwise turn. It took more force than he remembered when drilling it, but he heard, and felt, the click of its release.

"Don't forget to close the valve," Stewart said.

John berated himself, then ran his fingers up the line and found the valve. A simple switch he only had to push into place, then back, after he attached the new feed. He had to remind himself to take his time and check everything first. Once he was sure the line was ready, he unhooked the first bag, then put the coupler for the new one in place.

He felt a smile on his face as the coupler clicked together. He flicked the switch for the valve and opened it back up to continue receiving the plasma. John allowed himself a brief moment to appreciate the advances in medicine that had come with first contact. The ability to artificially create plasma for injuries that needed an infusion had saved countless lives over the years.

The ricochet of a bullet brought him back to the present with a jolt. Stewart's hand found his shoulder and was shoving him down over George's body. He tried to look up, though at the moment he wasn't sure why. He really didn't want to see the business end of the weapon that would kill him.

What greeted him was a darkly armored combat suit with a reflective dome. It was moving towards them with its weapon raised, pointed squarely at his face. John's breath caught in his throat as his blood ran cold, it was Shezlan. He knew he was about to die, and the sour thought of his news outlet using the footage from his helmet camera to portray the story, crossed his mind.

"Get away from my team you furry bastard!"

The reverberations of automatic fire suddenly shook John's body. He felt the presence of someone jumping over him and saw them land in a kneeling pose. He watched in fascination as the oncoming Shezlan tried to attack the newcomer, only to be pelted by repeated fire from the operator's rifle.

As the Shezlan went down in a heap, John looked up at his savior. He allowed himself to realize it was a tad melodramatic, but he didn't care. Somehow, he was unsurprised when it was Keith standing there.

"Can't get any footage from down there, Newsie."

"Yeah," John replied with an unsteady huff.

"How's George?"

"He's stable," Stewart answered, "but he needs medevac."

"Call it in," Keith ordered.

John shook himself and grabbed Stewart's arm, "You need help?"

Stewart nodded, "Yep, we'll have to carry him to the hangar."

"When you can move," Keith added.

John glanced up and tried to think what he meant by that, "When we can move him?"

"When all the enemies are dead."

John blinked, then the sound of battle reached his ear as he turned off his hearing protection. The rest of First Squad was still exchanging fire with the Shezlan he had seen coming behind them. He couldn't understand how they were all still fighting, all the gun fights he had seen had been over quickly.

"Why are they holding so tight?"

Keith shrugged, "I don't know, man."

"Alright," Stewart said, "Newsie, you and I will carry him out when it's go time."

John nodded, "Just say when."

As Keith moved away, John went back to looking at the drone camera. Now, he could see a large part of the promenade and blanched at the scene. The bodies and the debris from all the fighting lay strewn about in some haphazard display. It was as if a toddler had tossed out all their toys then went to play somewhere else.

"Mind on the here and now, Newsie," Stewart said as he worked.

John looked back to him as he worked on George, "How do you guys do this all the damn time?"

"Do what?"

"Get into these ridiculous fights? Dance with death? Take your pick."

"You're going to ask me this now?" Stewart asked with a laugh, "In the thick of it?"

"Humor me."

"Someone has to," he replied, "someone has to chase the monsters away, and in my case, someone has to look after those who do."

"That's it?"

"You were expecting poetry?"

John shrugged, "Well I mean..."

"Hey man, look at it this way. No matter why we started this, each of us lives for the moment of calm, for the peace when it's not popping off."

John considered that, and as he was about to ask another question, Stewart got up and went to inspect the Shezlan. He first thought Stewart was going to do what he had seen all the others do, put another shot in them. Instead, he watched Stewart do the same check over he had seen him giving George.

"Um, what was that?"

"All part of the oath," Stewart said.

"Even to the enemy who just tried to kill you?"

Stewart nodded, "I'm not really sure how many people stop and think about that."

"I'd say less than you give credit for."

"You're probably right, but that doesn't change the fact."

John had to admit he agreed, and in a small way, it was refreshing. After seeing how the initial fighting had gone, he wasn't sure there was room for empathy on the team. Maybe he was being too harsh, but it was a strange dynamic.

"You thinking about the follow up shots?"

John laughed, "You a telepath now?"

"Just experienced," Stewart replied, "it's a common enough thought."

"Alright, so explain it."

"Survival on the battlefield. Any of them can pick a weapon up and get back into the fight. Be it by picking up a weapon or clacking off a grenade."

"Oh."

Stewart patted his shoulder and despite the battle he could hear going on, he felt himself relax. John couldn't decide if it was helpful or not, but he knew it was something he had to consider. So many moving parts to his story. He supposed there would need to be tough questions addressed, even if they weren't what he exactly planned at first.

His eyes went to the drone footage, he could see Keith still holding his position at the other entry to the promenade. There was no more shooting, but he was still pointing his rifle down the corridor. When he looked to the others fighting the Shezlan, he saw they had moved back to different cover, still fighting, but further into the promenade than before.

"What's going on over there Six?" Came Keith's voice.

"Just some housekeeping," replied Harrison.

"One-one," came Silverling's voice, "this is one-three. They aren't pushing. It's like they just want to keep us locked in a firefight."

Granberg's rumbling voice came next, "Something's up one-one, I can feel it."

"Alright," Keith's voice had an edge John wasn't sure he liked "Stop playing nice. How are we on swarmers?"

"Out."

"Frags?"

The silence on the line felt like an eternity to John. Deep down, he wondered why they hadn't used a grenade yet, but he also expected they had used them all in the open space of the promenade. The fact Keith was asking was strange to him and when he looked at Stewart, he received a head shake at the unasked question.

"I've got three over here," Silverling said, "and three flashbangs, but that's an awfully confined space that isn't rated for a blast this big. No fire suppression system yet, and several places still open to vacuum."

"I know," Keith replied, "authorization given. Flash and blast Pew-Pew."

16

Eversley checked the latch on his harness one last time, then nodded to Holte. She looked over the rail, for what he thought had to have been the tenth time, and finally gave a thumbs up. He kicked off and back, free-falling for just an instant before his belaying cable stopped his descent.

As he worked to stabilize his movement, he spared a glance down to the ground where George had fallen. He could see Newsie and Stewart beside the man, still doing first aid. Eversley let out a soft prayer, then focused on a stable descent to the tower.

Once his feet contacted the roof of the promenade's tower, he activated the magnetic grip on his boots. The tower's dome top was likely slick, and he had no desire to take the express line down. He unhooked his harness and moved towards the top of the arch, to a point he and Silverling had designated for breach.

"Area clear," he said into the com. "Getting ready to deploy the charge."

He glanced up, saw the other fast ropes sail out to the open space, and his squad started their descent. Most of them anyway. Bekele and Turgenev were watching the descent with their coil guns. The massive weapons were not going to join in the breach, he and Holte decided they'd be better served going to First Squad.

Eversley pulled out three magnetic anchors and placed them in a triangular fashion, three feet apart. He then laced a thin cord of explosive material, a special mix Silverling made for him to use. He suspected it was a thermite, a material that would burn through most metals in spectacular fashion.

"You sure you set this up right?" Holte asked him as she approached.

Eversley shrugged, "Guess we'll see."

"Cause that helps me feel better," she grumbled.

Andrews cut in, "Let's pop this off. All this waiting is getting me trigger happy."

"Fire in the hole!"

Eversley clicked the remote for the detonators and the cord vanished in a bright, hot flash. The material had burned through the surface plating and supports, all the way into the room beyond. As the trio panned their rifles in the space, they could see no one present, no one on guard.

"Alright, here we go," Eversley said as he dropped in.

He looked left to right as he moved toward the door, listening for Holte and Andrews to drop in behind him. After only three steps, he heard Holte, then Andrews by the time he reached the door. The room was not large, by any means, compact with sensors and an auxiliary monitoring station.

"Clear," he called softly.

Moments later, a similar call came from his two companions as they stacked up against him. With them in place, Eversley reached for the override handle on the door, put in place for power failure; it worked to carefully slide the door away as well. His muzzle moved out of the space and into the stairwell that led down to the tower's office areas.

Eversley moved forward, minding each step, not wanting to find some trap as he went. The approach was agonizingly slow as the door to the interior of the tower came closer. He also worried that a worker, or Shezlan, would step into the stairwell.

"Eversley," Holte whispered, "when we get there, point your sighting mount at the door."

Eversley nodded, "Sure thing. You got the feed?"

"Yup."

Eversley eased forward, pointing his rifle at the center of the door. He thumbed the switch to activate his weapon's multifunction sight. The only thing left to do was to wait at the door while his team scanned the area beyond.

"Are you sure the door is thin enough and not shielded?" asked Andrews.

"Doubtful," Holte answered. "It's nothing important, just an access door to a backup station."

"They probably treat it like a janitor's closet," Eversley added.

He waited with his finger hovering just against his trigger. The idea of someone coming through kept appearing in his mind as he played the 'what if' game. Keith had always encouraged it, but never at the expense of the moment, and Eversley was understanding why even more.

"Two tangos," Holte said, breaking his thoughts.

"About halfway down the hall," Andrews added. "They aren't straying too far from that door."

Eversley felt a smile creep onto his face, "I bet we can call jackpot."

"Let's not get too hyped," Holte cautioned. "Mind on the fight."

"Copy."

"Good," she said, "they are standing on the left and right side of the hall, facing each other. Looks like an argument. Ready on you Two-two."

Eversley took a long, steady breath as Andrews moved up and got ready to open the door. It was simple enough, release the latch and push. Eversley felt Holte press up against his back as well, her rifle over his left shoulder, making it clear who she'd take.

Eversley gave a nod, and the door slid away from the latch, surprisingly silent. As it opened fully, he aimed at the individual on the right, a dark-haired male, and squeezed the trigger of his laser. The near instantaneous beam of energy burned the air, crackling, and then sizzling as it struck the man in the head.

He watched both fall to the floor in a heap, and as soon as Holte's pressure was off his back, Eversley moved forward. The urge to rush was boiling through his skin, but he kept his movement calm and orderly. Slow was smooth, smooth was fast.

Each space between them and the room they were heading to was a potential hiding place for an enemy. He and Holte cleared some sort of office while Andrews watched the hall. 'Holding security', as the saying went. Eversley suspected they used the office as a staging area before the fighting had started. Scattered shells and ammunition pouches littered the space.

As he and Holte exited, he noticed Andrews kneeling at an elevator door. He was placing a block to keep the doors from closing and was reaching in to pull the emergency stop. Eversley hissed at him, and when Andrews looked back, he shook his head.

"If they still have someone monitoring, they'd see an emergency stop," Holte added.

Andrews nodded and stomped the wedge into the track. Eversley smirked and moved forward. The distinct scent of laser-scored flesh was evident as they closed in on the two bodies. He kept his muzzle pointed at the one he shot, not wanting to be mistaken that he hadn't killed them.

"Mine's down hard," Holte said.

Eversley nodded, "Same here."

"Set the sensor at the door."

Eversley did as ordered and pointed his sighting system at the door, just as before. He stayed to the side now since he had some space to move. The mental images of someone opening this door were less troubling, because now he'd have a chance to react.

"I've got one on the floor and cold," Holte said, "one leaning against the wall by the door, and one kneeling by the one on the floor. Far side of the room, no weapons to be seen."

"Likely Bingo," Andrews chimed in as he pointed down the hall.

"Open, clear, and don't shoot anyone," Holt directed. "Andrews take the one on the wall. Eversley and I will push up on the ones across the room."

Eversley nodded, and after glancing at the others, he used the override handle to open the door. Andrews moved in ahead of him, then deeper into the room; Holte on his heels as he crossed the distance. His weapon was still leveled at the people he was approaching.

"Stay there," he commanded, "show me your hands."

The man in front of him looked terrified, falling back to his rump, hands rising. He was rambling about something, but it was hardly coherent. Eversley didn't care at that moment, only that there was no threat. He reached out, grabbed the man's shoulder, and rolled him over as he searched him for weapons.

"Clear," He called.

Soon Andrews added, "Clear here."

"Clear here," Holte said. "Two-one for overwatch, sending you photo for verification and identification."

Eversley waited tensely for the response from Jubert. The ideas running through his head, of this being a ploy, were going crazy. The thought did occur that, if this was the V.I.P, he was pointing his weapon at the leader of the Tronis government.

"Overwatch for two-one," Jubert answered. "V.I.P.'s confirmed."

Eversley chuckled and patted the man on the shoulder, "Sorry Sir. Rules."

"I'm hardly going to complain," Director Hawthorne said uneasily.

Eversley stood and offered the man a hand up, "Let's get you moving to safety."

"Not without them," Director Hawthorn demanded, as he pointed to the man Andrews had and the woman on the floor.

"Living first sir," Eversley said firmly.

The man was about to argue, but the other man by the wall interrupted him, "Sir, please. I'll stay behind with her, but you must go."

"Gentlemen," Holte snapped, "it's not up for debate. I'm sorry, but this is how it is. Once we have more control of the situation, we will come back for her."

Eversley breathed a sigh of relief as the Director relented. He understood the issue, the reasoning, for not wanting to leave a fallen comrade on the field. The situation was too fluid though, and until the station was safe, any fallen would have to wait for evacuation.

"Two-one for all elements," Holte called over the com. "Bingo, say again, Bingo."

"Overwatch for Two-one, we copy Bingo. Exfil will be checkpoint Sierra. Say again, exfil is checkpoint Sierra."

"Good copy," Holte replied. "Eversley, you're on point. Andrews, rear security."

Eversley turned and moved out of the room, making for the elevator they had locked up. While the fastest route down, he knew it was the most dangerous. There was every chance the enemy would try to lock down the elevator once they knew what was up. He also knew that Jubert had access to the system, so he could override it and just send them nonstop to the promenade.

Eversley cued his mic, "Two-two for One-one. How's the situation in the promenade?"

"One-one here," came Keith's voice, "good to hear you. The situation is isolated to our entry point. Opposition seems—"

Eversley blinked, waiting for what felt like an eternity. He glanced at his HUD and saw his radio was still working. He gave it another moment before getting back on the com line.

"Two-two for One-one, I did not copy your last. Opposition is what?"

The com stayed silent, and he felt his heart start pounding. Keith never left him hanging this long on the line. His mind raced all the different scenarios, and it took effort to get his mind on a back-up plan to get out.

"Two-two for Two-one," he said into the com, "I can't make contact with First Squad. Going to recon directly."

"You be careful."

"Always," he replied.

"Yeah, bullshit," Holte said.

He removed the block and hit the button to go down. Once the door closed, it was a swift and smooth descent. Eversley took advantage of the moment, swapping out his laser rifle for his friend's ballistic rifle.

The doors opened, thankfully on the promenade floor, and he burst out, looking for a threat. He was greeted with several bodies. Armed station workers turned terrorists. The room was perforated with bullet holes, and with experience Eversley understood, they were from railgun fire.

"Two-two for any Gamma element," he said. "I'll be exiting the promenade's tower."

"Good copy," came Stewart's voice, "come on out."

Eversley moved out of the building with haste, but control. He went right to the waving hands of Newsie and Stewart. He skidded to a stop on his knees next to them.

"Glad you could make it," Stewart chuckled.

"And miss all this?"

17

John had to resist the urge to laugh at Eversley's arrival. The man had an absurd smile, despite all that was going on. He wasn't sure what was more entertaining, the smile or the slide on his knees the last ten feet, it reminded him of a soccer player celebration.

Though John had to admit, he wasn't sure celebration was the right emotion. The sounds of gunfire had stopped, but no one had been saying anything. The silence on the radio, and in the surrounding air, gave him goosebumps.

"What's the situation, brother?" Eversley asked Stewart.

John noticed Eversley didn't speak loudly. The conversation was barely a whisper, as if any loud sound would break the silence. He had a pit forming in his stomach as he endured it all.

"I don't know man," Stewart whispered. "The shooting stopped and, it's like a switch got flipped."

John looked at his drone feed, and with his mouth dry, moved the drone so he could see the area of battle. As the drone panned around, his heart nearly leapt into his throat. He couldn't see any of the team at the battle site. The crates and barricades were shot to pieces, but still standing. No one was there though.

"Where did they go?" John asked.

He blinked, realizing both Stewart and Eversley were looking at him. The intensity they both possessed in that moment almost made him as uneasy as Holte could. Then again, he couldn't imagine anyone more intimidating, even in the midst of this ordeal.

"Dude," Eversley snapped, "share."

"Oh! Umm... they aren't there, no one is."

"The fuck?"

Eversley and Stewart exchanged looks. John felt some secret language pass between them. Eversley hopped to his feet, and crouch walked his way towards the corridor in question. John started to turn, but Stewart stopped him and pulled a collapsible litter out of the medical kit.

"Are we just going to risk going to the checkpoint?"

Stewart shook his head. "No, I want to be ready to roll though. Holte and the rest of Second should be coming down soon."

"Then we all mad-dash to Sierra?"

Stewart nodded as he worked, the litter taking shape in just a few snaps of the braces. The canvas being fed out from the poles they'd use as handles. John briefly wondered if it was sturdy, but the confidence the medic was showing in it erased the thought as fast as it came.

"Alright," Stewart directed, "you come grab his legs, I'll get his shoulder. We lift on three and sit him on the litter. Follow?"

John nodded and moved to where Stewart pointed. He squatted down, grabbed just at George's knees, and watched Stewart for his cue. The man nodded, counted out to three, and gave the command to lift. It surprised him at how easily the two of them could do so.

Once George was on the litter, he and Stewart raced to put straps in place. The process was intricate, and John was glad for the time Stewart had spent with him on it. They worked quickly and had everything ready by the time the radio call from Holte came.

"Two-One to any elements in the promenade. Are we clear?"

"This is One-four," Stewart said. "Area is clear."

John panned his drone and started to program it to follow the team. He had gotten pretty good at it and could put his attention back on what was happening. When Stewart motioned to him, he was already getting into place on the litter. He also turned on his helmet camera. On a subconscious level, he knew there would be some spectacular angles from it.

Holte and the rest of Second Squad came out of the doorway Eversley had earlier. Despite being told it was clear, they still had weapons out, looking for threats. He was less surprised by this than he expected to be and wondered if he hadn't been spending too much time around them all. He dismissed that thought immediately. There was no such thing as too much time around this team.

"Where'd Eversley run off to?" Holte asked as she got closer.

"He went to see what sort of trouble Chief got up to."

"Wonderful," Holte's voice dripped with sarcasm. "Alright, how's George?"

"He's stable and good to move."

Holte nodded, took one last glance around, and tapped John on the shoulder as she moved past. The rest of Second Squad formed around them and, with a nod from Stewart, he picked up his part of the litter. No sooner had he stood up straight did everyone start moving. He was by George's feet, letting Stewart lead the way and set the pace. John just hoped he could keep up.

He noticed beside him was Director Hawthorn and one of his security detail. The man looked haggard with down cast blood-shot eyes, and tears. John wasn't sure what to say, if anything was to be said. The man looked soul crushed if he had to pick a descriptor.

Holte led them down a corridor, taking them away from the promenade. They entered a slightly wider corridor, with various yellow caution lines painted on the floor and sides. John glanced and saw directional arrows lining the walls and floor as well. Any door they passed was wide and marked with color coded indicators. One of which, finally made it clear to John they used this as a cargo hall.

John almost forgot to look at his map on the HUD, and when he did, sucked in a breath. One door behind the team opened and several armed people in armor stepped out, weapons raised at their backs. He started to shout, but someone behind him was already doing so. His initial thought was to drop the litter and get out of the way.

"Keep going!" Holte barked, smacking Stewart on the shoulder as she turned and fired.

John didn't need to be told. He took his cue from what she had Stewart doing and kept his feet churning. He heard the eruption of weapons' fire as Holte and Andrews started firing at the attackers with a reckless spray of death. He spared a glance at the drone and saw the battle going on behind them. They were forcing the enemy back into the door.

"One-four to overwatch. Approaching Sierra, coming in hot!"

John looked back up and saw they were fast approaching a larger door. The indicators said it was a supply hangar. He almost let himself breathe a sigh of relief until a door to the side opened. He shouted at Stewart as he saw the muzzle of a rifle come out and started flashing. Plasma exploded against the wall and into Stewart's shoulder.

Stewart twisted away, drew a side arm John never noticed he carried, and started firing back. The security officer lunged forward, shoving the Director back into John as he went. He had to let go of the litter to try and keep his balance with the sudden addition of an extra body being shoved on him.

He managed to see the man dive-tackle the shooter, and push him into a second. The trio wrestled and battled for control of the rifle. Stewart was up now, and with his pistol, moved to fire into the space as well. Then John heard the shout that made his blood freeze.

"Grenade!"

Stewart dove away from the door, on top of him and the Director, shouting something. John tried to roll his back to the door, recalling something about the back plates being thicker. Then John remembered George and attempted to crawl over to the man, who lay exposed on the floor.

The fighting past the door was still happening, and he looked up in time to see the security officer smile at him. He was bleeding from stabs and cuts on his chest while being held by one of the Shezlan. He released a grenade to the floor and kicked the wall. John saw the door close just before the blast.

"Jacob!"

John was scrambling to his feet, looking back down to see Holte and Andrews running their way at a full sprint. Then, he saw Stewart using one arm to keep the Director from rushing to the door. He got up and ran over to help hold the man back.

"He's gone!" Stewart shouted. "We have to go!"

John wrapped his arms around the Director. "He's right. Jacob did his job. Don't make it wasteful."

He didn't know where the words came from, but they came. The fact he said it in a calm tone, was nearly as shocking. Something had changed, he knew that now, and made a mental note to explore if that was a good or bad thing.

When the others arrived, there was nothing said. Holte just grabbed the man and pulled him with her. Andrews helped Stewart up and jumped to his position on the litter. John took up his part and helped him, then moved as soon as he stood.

The large doors opened, and he saw the lander they came on sitting in the middle of the bay. The alarms were blaring, and John saw the wreckage of a ship he couldn't identify, slammed into the side of the bay. They pointed a large turret to the door behind him, large barrels spinning slowly, still smoking.

"Over watch to one-one. We have Second Squad and primary V.I.P.. Exfil site is compromised; recommend alternative exit."

"One-one copies all. New exfil."

John was relieved by one of the soldiers on the lander as he came in. They moved George to a place towards the front that served as a medical station. He noticed they were peeling Stewart's armor off as well, all while he was giving directions as to how to care for George.

The door closed behind them and Jubert moved past him, stopping to give him a pat on the shoulder. He suddenly felt less tired than he expected. He knew he had worked himself to the point of exhaustion, and felt the fatigue, but at the recognition it seemed to fade.

18

Eversley swapped out the last of his batteries for his laser rifle. The ballistic rounds were spent from his other weapon, and he had to strap it in place on his back. He adjusted the setting to near mid. It meant less initial impact power, but he could stay in the fight longer. Something that was becoming critical, even Turgenev and Bekelle were running low for their large coil guns.

He noticed Keith was looking at the layout of the station with Silverling. The radio traffic made things complicated. They had to change their plan to exit the station now. He didn't like the amount of 'on-the-fly' changes this mission had taken, but that was where the, "*deal with everything in between,*" comment Keith enjoyed so much, came from.

There was a sudden spike on his HUD, which caused his earpieces to scream static. He grunted out in pain at the audio assault on his ears. Glancing, he saw the others doing the same. Silverling had even tossed her helmet off. When the sound subsided, Keith planted it back into her chest with an angry glare.

"What the fuck was that?" Eversley asked.

"No idea," Keith said, "but I am in no hurry to find out. We've got a path. Let's get going."

Eversley blinked, and shook his head, trying to yawn or something to clear the sound. It felt like it was echoing inside his head still. Things sounded muffled and distorted as he and everyone moved. That is until Silverling stopped the squad.

"Hey...chief...," she said in that drawn out sort of way he hated so much.

"What's up Pew-Pew?"

"I've got a hit on my sentry system."

Eversley blinked. "Why'd you turn that on?"

Silverling shrugged. "Wanted to watch for booby-traps."

"Are we getting close to one?" Keith asked.

"No, but that's the issue."

"Explain why this is relevant, please," Keith pressed.

"Okay, so the system actively scans for nearby radio triggers, infrared, or explosive material. Then, lets me know when we get near something like that. Range is limited to about twenty meters. Follow?"

Keith nodded and made a motion with his hands, "Waiting on the punch line."

"Alright so, that signal scrambled the unit but when it cleared up, the explosives detector picked up traces of uranium."

"That's not a booby-trap. That's a going away package," Eversley said.

Keith nodded, "One-one to Overwatch. Code Mako. I say again, Code Mako."

There was silence on the line that made the hair on Eversley's neck stand on end. The idea of a nuclear device on the station brought all sorts of problems. Then, the big question, how long did they have until it went boom?

"Mako Confirmed," came Jubert's voice. "Protocol demands we move off to a safe distance, doubly due to our V.I.P.."

"Understood," Keith said.

Eversley wanted to swear again. They had just been told they had no ride out of here. The protocol was absolute, and in place for good reason, but he liked it even less than he had before. He wasn't sure how Keith was going to get them out of this one.

"Alright," he said. "What's the play Chief?"

Keith pointed to Silverling, "Can you trace the material?"

Silverling shrugged, "Maybe but, it'd be easier if we tie it into the station's monitoring system."

"Alright," Keith said. "Eversley, find me a monitoring station we can tie into."

Eversley pulled up the station map and started looking. He was starting to wish the notes had the active sites marked. Hunting for one cold like this was a pain of unequaled annoyance.

"The rest of you listen up," Keith was saying, "we will continue pursuing the Shezlan who fell back. I'm betting they have an exit in mind. This is why they broke contact. Silverling, Eversley and Granberg will get to the monitoring station and find the bomb."

"We are sure it's a bomb?" Turgenev asked.

"Has to be. The Shezlan, or the insurgents, want the station disrupted. Failing their hostage protection, they'd plan to blow it. The team we were fighting with just cut and run, that's pull out tactics one-o-one."

"Found one, just two junctions away," Eversley called out.

"Good. Get going."

Eversley shared the path, and the three broke off, running down the indicated hallway. The path wasn't overly far from where he had pegged the course of the Shezlan team. He knew Keith would be on the hunt; they'd need intel and information.

There was also the fact, they had an escape plan. They could use that.

He felt like he was moving too fast, the old axiom was counter to what he was doing. The imagined pressure of a clock just made it worse. He was running against an invisible opponent, and that just made his skin crawl.

There was also the issue of his team running into an angry team of Shezlan in an ambush. The Fire Team, with only half of its members present, would face difficulty when confronted by them. The saving grace, he thought, was that the Shezlan were likely in bug-out mode. They probably wouldn't want a drawn out fight when they could just hot foot it to their exfil.

He slid around the corner and planted his arm on the wall to keep himself upright as they closed in on the objective. *Almost there, almost to the finish line; just a few more strides.* The next turn came into sight, and he forced himself to slow. He glanced back down the hall and saw Silverling and Granberg skidding to a halt several strides back.

"I swear, running is in his DNA," Silverling said to Granberg.

He grunted in reply as they came up to him and moved the last few feet to the door. Now, they were moving with speed, but control. This close to their objective, there were so many things that could go wrong, and they had already broken some serious rules. Now in the home stretch, one needed to be smart.

They opened the door and breached the room orderly and quietly. No surprises, but he knew Keith would have been proud of how smooth it went. Then came the complicated part, getting tied into the system.

Silverling set to work, giving he and Granberg orders on what to open and connect. Not five minutes later, they had the sentinel system, using the station's internal monitoring sensors, working for them. He held his breath as he watched her work out the details between the networks.

He started pacing, looking at monitors, seeing if he could make out the details. He was only passingly familiar with how the system worked and that was not helping with his frustration. He imagined a radio call for help to come in at any moment. He wanted to help and speed it up, but Silverling had it in hand.

"Got it!"

Eversley spun and moved over to where she was standing. The monitor in-front of her was flashing an indicator in the station's core. The concentration was registering red and orange, with various icons on the screen, around where it was sitting.

"Is there a camera there we can access?" He asked.

A moment later, a monitor came on, and he could see a large rectangular box. It was laying in the midst of several large pipes and conduits. The space looked like a service station for the area; everything made a junction around it and there was a catwalk.

"Where is that?"

"Freight core," Silverling explained, "near the central line. Makes sense, that's probably the best area for maximum propagation."

"If it's nuclear, what does it matter?"

"It may not be nuclear," she explained.

"With uranium?"

"Thyla," she explained, "is rich in uranium. They've been using it long before we had, development wise. It's likely not nuclear in the classic sense."

"That's reassuring."

"Probably closer to a dirty bomb from the twentieth and twenty-first on Earth. Except they use the uranium as fuel, like we would Symtex."

"Fuck too. It's still a nuke."

She shrugged. "Either way, it's not far. Just a section towards the core."

"Can you disarm it?"

She nodded. "Yep, just get me there."

"Granberg, new location," he called.

The man grunted and was already moving out, Silverling on his heels. Eversley looked at the screen again before heading out. He keyed his mic as they started another sprint.

"Two-two for one-one. Objective located. Moving to secure."

"Good copy," Keith replied, "and good luck."

"You too."

The race was on once again, and they tore down the hallway. Eversley was overtaking the other two every stride. Silverling was the only one who ever gave him a challenge on running days, and even she was hard pressed to keep the lead she had.

They found the access hatch easily enough, and the situation slowed down again. This, he was sure, would be a dangerous place. One glance at the door and he knew they were going to have problems. The welding job was professional, and if it weren't for the fact they were about to get blown up, he'd have complimented it.

"Can you breach and not set off the bomb?"

Silverling was already examining the door and nodding. She had a detector in her hand and was working around the door frame, marking different places with notes on the wall. A laser cutter was in her hand, eating its way through part of the door.

"Let me get a peek first," she said. "I'll know more when I get a better look."

Eversley advised the rest of the team and Jubert of the situation. As the affirmative came back, he felt his heart in his chest again. He had to sit and wait, letting his teammate do the work. She was second to none, and he had all the faith in the world, but he hated the wait.

Time ticked by at a distorted rate. He knew it wasn't long, but it felt like it was taking forever. He checked the chronometer on his HUD, counting clusters of seconds as if they were minutes. The entire process was taking too long, something in the back of his mind was screaming to be anywhere else but there.

"I'm through," Silverling announced.

Eversley spun back and watched her feeding her camera in the hole. The feed came to his wrist device, and he watched the camera bend back to look at the door. She identified a booby trap against the wall, then looked at the bomb, snaking across the way quickly. The view shifted as the camera started to slink up the side of the crate holding the bomb.

"Well, this is pretty standard," She explained. "Looks like a timer and a remote trigger."

Eversley looked at her, "You are way too calm saying that."

"Hey, if it's gonna go boom before I get it stopped, we won't be here to care."

"Fuck too," Eversley muttered.

Silverling laughed, "Oh, live a little."

"That's kind of what I'm hoping for," he replied. "Granberg, back me up here!"

Granberg looked at them both, then just muttered and grumbled under his breath.

"We are all about to die, and that's all you have to say?"

Granberg shrugged in response.

"Overwatch to all elements," came Jubert's commanding voice. "We just monitored a ship blasting out of the lower hangar bay."

"Eversley," Silverling's voice had an edge to it, "The timer just clicked on."

"How long?"

"I don't read *furball*," she snapped. "Likely the time it'd take to get to a safe distance, so minutes."

"Two-two for all," he snapped on the com. "The device just went active, no idea of exact time."

Jubert's voice came again, "Evac now, this mission is eight ball. Say again, eight ball."

"One-one to all elements still on station, rally my location. Double time."

"You heard the man, "Eversley barked, "Move it!"

19

John couldn't believe what he was hearing. "How are they getting out?"

"Not now, Newsie," Holte snapped.

He turned and saw the same comment written in the expression on Jubert's face. The man's eyes narrowed slightly, and his jaw clenched. Since director Hawthorne had been recovered, the man had been on edge. John never expected the commander to be unsettled by anyone.

"Tell them to stop the bomb," Hawthorne ordered.

"They have no idea how much time it has," Jubert snapped back. "It's also behind a welded shut, and booby-trapped, door. I can guarantee you, there is no time. Now sit down and stop talking."

"That station is an asset of my government commander," he countered, "or did you forget that?"

"Your authority vanished when you were taken hostage and won't be returned," Jubert replied, "until returned home and given a full medical and psychological evaluation. That doesn't change. Now stop talking."

John was glad his visor was darkened still, otherwise the smirk he felt growing on his face would be obvious. News reporters made enemies as easily as friends, maybe a little easier. He had no desire to have the Director of Tronis on his list of enemies just because he thought it was funny the man got checked.

It faded though, he looked out the observation window and saw the station still steadily shrinking behind them. Holte had explained that since they had the director on board, they had to make sure he was as safe as possible. That meant not being anywhere near the range of a potential nuclear bomb. The operators on the station were expendable, the V.I.P. was not.

"How far away is another ship that can get them?" John asked.

Andrews shook his head. "Couple of hours. They built the station for optimal placement between the jump points into the system. Not so much for the colony."

"How long do you think they have?"

"Well," Andrews said, "I'd say ten minutes. Long enough for the escape craft to get to a safe distance. They didn't even bother trying to engage us, they just went; so I'd bet it's a short timer."

"Everything a bet to you?"

"Normally."

John shook his head. They all seemed to deal with things differently, and it seemed Andrews took bets on how things would go. He wondered just how the man ever planned on getting paid as he would bet on the worst outcomes. He chalked it up to that dark humor Keith had told him about once.

"You just ready to accept their fate?"

Andrews shook his head. "Until it happens, it hasn't happened. I'm not sure what Keith has in mind, but I'll be shocked if it doesn't work."

"That's a lot of faith to place on the man."

"When you've been up to your eyes in the shit as much as he has, it's clear you've got someone looking out for you."

"You're placing the lives of your team in the hands of an imaginary guardian angel?"

"Not one for faith?"

John shook his head. "I think it's clear there isn't a God. Just look at this situation, or the universe in general."

Andrews shrugged. "I'm not sure about that, but I'm also not sure, it's an angel. Could be a demon that just enjoys Keith's brand of chaos."

John rolled his eyes. "Because that's going to make things better."

Andrews laughed and patted him on the shoulder. John knew deep down the man was probably just as worried, he just had a way to deal with it. It made little sense, but then again, nothing typically did around Gamma. They just sort of did their own thing and ran with it.

Keith's voice came over the com line, "One-one for Overwatch. We have an evac solution, but need some help."

John spun and looked towards Jubert, then noticed his camera was still on from before. He shrugged and settled in to watch what was about to happen. Difficult times meant it was time to simply be a reporter, and document the story.

"This is Overwatch," Jubert said. "What have you got?"

"We are just going to jump. We've found a small maneuvering device."

"Copy. That won't get you past the safety limit in any sort of rush."

"I know, but it gets us off the station and maybe someone could pick us up on the way by?"

"I'll see what I can scrounge up."

John let out a sigh, "Are we going to pick them up?"

Jubert looked at him and shook his head. "Nope, can't close inside the safety line."

"So, who is going to pick them up?"

Jubert smiled, "We can't go inside the safe distance, however, I have two Tigersharks as escorts."

John nodded, "Yea, but they don't have a passenger bay."

"They don't need one, they can just hang on to the exterior."

"They can do that?"

"Zero gravity and zero atmosphere lets you do more than you think."

Hawthorne stormed back from the cabin. "Those are Tronis Defense Force property, you can't order them to do anything."

"Watch me."

Jubert turned away from the director and stepped towards the communication console again. Hawthorne tried to follow, but Holte intercepted him with an audible growl. The Director glared, but said nothing and went back to his seat.

"Gamma Overwatch to escorts. I need someone brave."

The com crackled back to life, "Copy that. What can we do for you?"

"That you, Blackout?"

"One and only, my man. What can the Tronis Space Corpse do for the UN?"

Jubert chuckled, "Just a quick pickup of my team. They will be space jumping from the station and need a ride out of the safe distance."

"You mean, risk being blown up by a nuclear bomb to pick up hitchhikers?"

"Yep."

"You realize that could be a one-way trip."

"I do. To quote one of my men though, 'No balls'. You going to let that stand?"

"Oh, hell no! Tell your folks their ride is inbound."

Jubert nodded, closed the line, then relayed the news to Keith and the others. John made sure to zoom in on the smile the man had as he did so. When he looked over at Andrews, the man's expression said it all. "*Told you so.*"

John sat down at one of the multi-use workstations and found a way to tie into the feed from one of the Tiger Shark's external targeting cameras. He couldn't control it, but he was hoping it could get some sort of footage. There was also the fact he wanted to see what was happening. Sitting on the lander was safe, but very disconnected.

"There they are," John said, louder than he intended.

He felt Holte and the others press around him as the fast attack craft closed in on their teammates. They could be seen as faint discolorations against the void at first, but became clear as Blackout closed in on them. There were friend or foe markers on the screen as their combat suits linked up to the Tiger Shark's targeting system.

"What's all this?" John asked as he pointed to the red targeting reticle.

Holte leaned in and looked, "It's a target lock. He's plotting an intercept."

She pointed on the screen to the indicators and the ever shifting, dotted lines that Blackout must have been using. The lines merged at a point ahead of the team, while the merger was moving closer and closer to the team. Her free hand was squeezing his shoulder, and even through the armor, he could feel pressure.

"Come on," Holte whispered, "just a bit more."

John's mouth felt dry, "They'll make it right?"

"As long as that bomb doesn't blow," Andrews snarked.

"How do you joke about this?"

"It's how I cope."

Holte nodded, "I'd like to say he's lying, but he's not."

John just continued to watch, the camera was staying focused on the team. They were able to watch as the Tiger Shark was now in front of them and getting in line. The dotted line vanished as he watched one of the team release the machine that had taken them that far. Someone else reached for the side of the ship.

He could see that cables were connecting everyone, and one by one, they were being pulled close to grasp onto something. They clipped to anything they could find and then one, John assumed it was Keith, gave a thumbs up to the camera. The Tigershark then accelerated. He looked at different panels and finally found the radar showing the ship as it approached the safe distance line.

"Massive energy spike detected!"

John looked up, trying to see who spoke. Whoever it was, they were lost in the controlled chaos that was suddenly happening. Everyone moved toward seats. Andrews dragged him towards one, strapped him in, then the man leapt back to one of his own.

"What the hell?"

"No idea how big it is," Andrews said. "We aren't sticking around."

John looked at the monitor and swore, "They're so close."

"They'll be fine."

He felt a shifting of the craft, then heard the engine roar to life as the lander went to maximum acceleration. Everyone was feeling the pressure as the G-force increased, and the ship threatened to leave them behind. In almost the same instant, the ship shook as the speakers called out a warning.

"Detonation!"

John didn't need the screen, he could see out the observation window as the station suddenly broke in half. A flash of white, thankfully filtered by his helmet, and then a massive flash of orange and white as the station exploded. It was disturbing, how silent it was. No sound due to no atmosphere, that also meant the fireball was massive. It looked as if a second sun suddenly appeared in the system as all the fuel, oxygen, and sheer force of a bomb, coalesced into something roughly spherical.

20

Eversley could feel the heat on his back, even through the suit's armor and temperature regulation. Nothing was really designed to regulate what was happening behind them. It felt like he had leaned against a giant shell casing; a searing, short-lived burn that was just pure heat.

There wasn't anything of substance to hold on to, just the lip of the wing. He was still attached to the others with the cable, but he really wished he could have an anchor point on the ship. Thankfully, some of them did, so none of them were going anywhere. *If they didn't fry like an egg.*

He briefly thought back to his days in basic training and recalled nothing like this on the list of things they'd been trained for. As his mind drifted back, images of his son came to him; playing with small toys, eventually getting big kid toys and the like. The smile on his face when he got told he could live with dad full time.

There was a feeling on the top of his hand, pressure intermittently. He glanced over and saw Qureshi had a grip in his hand. Their coms were crackling, so he couldn't hear anything, and it appeared she couldn't either. She smiled briefly, then closed her eyes and said something. He didn't need to hear to know she was praying, and while different in faith, he joined her.

The isolation in the helmet was distorting as the only sound was his own breathing. He wasn't sure how many prayers he had gone through, time seemed skewed. While he knew it was just a trick of the mind, it still felt like an eternity. Then, the com crackled back to life and a flood of sound and voices came to him; Jubert, Blackout, Keith, Newsie, and even Holte.

"I'm good," he repeated.

"One-one for all," came Keith's voice, "All present and accounted for. We're okay."

Eversley looked out towards the void all around them, then smiled. The end hadn't come, and everything else in the universe didn't even notice all their antics. It brought a sense of calm that he sorely felt he needed at the moment.

"Allah still has need of us in the universe," Qureshi said on a one-to-one channel.

Eversley laughed, "God isn't ready to put up with us just yet, is more likely the case."

She laughed and nodded, "Perhaps. Until then, I am glad I've got my brother along for the work Allah has for me."

"Always got your six, little sis."

Harrison piped up over the com, "So, now what?"

"We get comfortable," Keith said, "It'll be a long flight back to Tronis and one of their orbital stations."

"Anyone got some cards?"

Harrison countered, "You know that program cheats, right?"

"You just say that, because you lose all the time."

"Alright," Keith interrupted, "Now that we aren't immediately going to die, let's get better secured on this thing."

The process took time, which was good, as Eversley had something to focus on. Everything had to be done in tandem, and methodically; one hand on the line, one hand on the craft. The beauty and curse of being in zero gravity worked in their favor this time. Through determination and teamwork, they were finally secured enough to the Chief's standards. Eversley napped the rest of the way, earning a semi restful, dreamless sleep.

The next thing he knew, they were getting ready to land on what passed for an orbital defense station. The landing bay was large enough for the transport and the two Tiger Sharks, not much else. As soon as the doors closed, what space there was suddenly had deck crew rushing in to secure the craft and get Gamma off the Tiger Shark.

They rushed Eversley out the door and down the hall to a medical station, where they stripped away his armor. A pair of doctors probed and prodded him, and while he winced at each touch, he was relieved they were being gentle. A cream was being applied and soothing relief flowed from it, feeling ice cold in counter to the searing heat he felt before.

"Well, you won't have to go to the beach for a tan anytime soon," said a nurse.

Eversley turned and looked at the younger man, "Going to give me the lecture about not tanning?"

"Would you listen?"

"Probably not."

"There's why. You and your team are all lucky. Much more exposure and you'd be hospitalized."

"Treat and release?"

"Yep."

"What do I owe ya?"

The nurse chuckled, "How about that brunette's number?"

"The one in the hijab?"

"No, but she is cute. I was meaning the one with 'Pew-Pew' on the shoulder."

Eversley laugh and hung his head, "Sorry dude, think she's hooked up with a reporter."

"Well damn. Alright, get out of here."

Eversley didn't wait for any further issues, he hopped off the table and pulled his shirt on. Stepping out into the hall, he saw many of the others, sitting along the floor, either sleeping or idly chatting amongst themselves. There was little pomp and circumstance to their return, just them and the walls.

"Well, did they say it's permanent?"

Eversley turned to see Keith walking towards him, "Is what permanent?"

"That ugly face of yours."

Eversley flipped the man off and grinned, "Naw, they weren't worried about perfection man."

"Says you," Keith snarked, "You called Jason yet?"

Eversley shook his head, "No, just got cut loose."

Keith handed him a small terminal card, "Here, one right down the hall."

"Thanks man."

"No problem, brother," Keith smiled and gave him a fist bump.

Eversley wasted no time slipping past everyone, exchanging fist bumps or tiptoeing past as needed. Just as Keith had said there was a terminal in the hall, and it was open to use. He tapped the card to the screen and the network opened up, offering him five minutes of communication with a ten second delay.

"Damn Keith. Priority treatment," he muttered to himself.

Eversley noticed all the team's home contacts were on his list. He smiled, then pressed the one for Jason, and waited as the connection process started. It took time, after all it was a lot to get synced up and access to, but after about five minutes, he got a connection and heard the tone to start his message.

"Hey little man, just got back from a trip out. Wanted to see how you were enjoying grandma's and if you were being good for her. I've got a couple neat toys I'll bring you from here, and lots of awesome pictures."

He waited for the timer to click down as his son watched the message, then the video came back. His boy was sitting up in his bed by a window. It looked dark out and he instantly felt bad as he could see him rubbing his eyes.

"Hi daddy! I'm always good for Grandma; she always gives me an extra cookie and says so. I can't wait till you come home. We have kickball tomorrow, will you be back?"

Eversley felt his cheeks grow sore from the smile he knew he had. There was also the sting of tears as his vision blurred and he had to wipe them away. He composed himself the best he could, then started again.

"No, I won't make it back by then. That just means you will have to tell me about it when I do get home. I'm not sure just yet, but it will be soon. We just have to finish some things up. I'll let you get back to sleep. Love you, little man."

He waited for the exchange and the reply; it was fast and short. He chuckled as it played and even rewound it twice. He knew the line was closed, but he still said, "goodnight".

Eversley walked down the hall and paced around, finding an out of the way area to lean. He wanted to decompress, and there wasn't a good way here on the station. It would have to wait until they got to the surface, and there was no telling how long that would take.

"Wear a hole in the deck yet?" Holte asked.

"Naw," he replied, "you?"

She shook her head and stood across from him in the hall. They sat in silence for several minutes before looking at each other. He noticed Holte looked worried, and worn down more than usual.

"You alright?"

"Maybe," she said, "this deployment is getting to me. Keith had me running a squad twice now. I'm grateful, but almost losing you and George, that's more than I expected it to be."

"No doubt. You've done great all through it."

"Thanks buddy. I just don't know how he does it repeatedly."

"Maybe it's a Texas thing?"

"Yeah? And why aren't you that way?"

"Cause he has it covered."

They both laughed and lapsed into silence again. This time he didn't feel it was as oppressive, it was more peaceful and relaxing. To some degree, it was as soothing as going for a run.

"He doesn't get to quit or promote," she finally said.

"Just going to hold him hostage as team lead?"

"Yes."

He laughed, "Oh, I can't wait to see how that goes."

"You have to take over for my spot if he goes anywhere, buddy."

"Oh God, anything but that."

"See?"

"Alright, let's get back to the others," he finally said, "Make sure Newsie didn't puke."

They each laughed as they walked down the hall, and the others were coming out as well. Eversley exchanged some fist bumps and then gave Keith back his card in a handshake. He wasn't sure how many on the team got the privilege, and he was not going to out him.

Jubert stepped out and cleared his throat, "Listen up."

Eversley and the others fell silent and looked his way. He noticed the Commander looked worn out and half flustered. That worried him more than a bit, but if anyone could handle whatever had happened, it was Jubes.

"Intel will be collecting our vid files and wants reports by eight hundred hours, tomorrow morning. I pushed it back to twelve hundred hours. You all need to rest and decompress before reliving all that. It goes without saying, no discussion with anyone outside the squadron about this operation."

Eversley nodded, that made sense. Every operation had to have a hot wash, and they were never allowed to discuss things after the fact. Standard procedure was to pretend it never happened and be shocked when it finally made the light of day.

"Now the important part," Jubert said, "everyone is restricted to post when we get down to the base."

"Why?" Holte asked.

"Assistant Director Hall's request. She says there is a lot of uproar right now. The media, and several politicians, are pointing the finger at us as being negligent."

"That's a bunch of–" Eversley started.

"Enough," Jubert barked, "This is how it is. We work in the shadows, remember that. They don't get to know the whole story. They secured us a section on the station here to get some rest 'til they arrange our ride. Expect it to take a while. Dismissed."

Eversley and the others went as directed; Keith led the way to the section. He showed them the rooms that had been made available to them and then disappeared into a lift, which Eversley noticed had the U.N.I.S. guy in it. He shook his head, he knew Keith and felt sorry for him.

He surveyed the small space that had been assigned to him. It was small, dark, and smelly, but the bed was comfortable. That, above all else, he was thankful for as he sunk down onto it and fell back. He had just enough time to think how hard the pillow was, before drifting off to sleep.

21

John stared up at the ceiling, all the *wonderful* plain gray metal. He was exhausted, but his mind was still working, still churning the events over. This wasn't an unfamiliar state. He had worked on many stories over the years that had him thinking, instead of sleeping. They seldom involved so much violence, though.

He had been watching the news from the various centers on Tronis. The outlook on the operation and destruction of Avalon Station was all anyone could talk about. Each service talked non-stop about the amount of workers who had been assigned to the station, and likely killed, when it exploded.

Few talked about the T.D.F. team that had been sent to recover the Director, or the bomb. Those that did, mostly theorized about how it was due to the presence of military elements from Earth. The stories all seemed to leave out the Shezlan.

Director Hawthorne was expected to make a statement later in the night about the rescue operation and his return home. The look on his face when being led out of the hangar gave John the impression it wasn't going to be pretty. The man was likely to blame the T.D.F. for sending their own, instead of sending the specialized team from Earth. Then turn around and blame Gamma for not going back and stopping the bomb. He had long since turned it off by the end of that one.

There was a brief knock at his door before it slid open. A man in uniform stepped in and removed his hat. John recognized him immediately and groaned aloud. Just his luck, the colonel from U.N.I.S. was going to berate him.

"Hey, I'll be right there, just a moment," John said with more snark than he intended, but less than he wanted.

"Mister Aerovant," Shaikh replied in a calm, methodical tone, "I'm reasonably sure, I did not give you permission to go on this operation."

"I don't seem to recall needing to ask anyone other than Commander Jubert, and I certainly don't recall asking you about it."

"You realize I can arrest you for this stunt. Thereby, you'll lose all your access and authorization to speak about anything you observed during that time."

"Mister Shaikh," John started.

"Colonel," he corrected.

"Colonel," John said, "you've already tried the bully approach. How about you do us both a favor and give it a rest? I'm extremely tired. I am certain you have a mountain of things to do. Whatever it is you do with my footage, especially, given the presence of Shezlan soldiers in it."

"What Shezlan?"

John looked up, "You haven't..."

Shaikh looked at him flatly and John understood the question was more a statement. There would be no footage of them when he got it back. The footage would have their images computer wiped; either removing them entirely, or replacing them with insurgents in nondescript armor and helmets.

"You are absolutely incredible," John said with as much sarcasm as he could scrape up.

Shiekh shrugged and turned on the monitor on the wall. Unsurprisingly, it was on the news story about the raid, and subsequent destruction, of Avalon Station. The reporters were covering footage of demonstrations outside the military base and the capitol building of the colony.

"I am certain I said before," Shaikh said, "that people will take the truth to mean what they want it to and tell that story. Even though their own people were involved in the death of a long term public servant, and her security detail, they will blame Earth. They will lay the blame at Gamma Squadron's feet and not care about the truth."

John watched the footage as it panned from one protest to the next. People holding signs telling the military to go away. Calling the Tronis government, 'collaborators with Earth'. Families left to grieve as their loved ones were on the station, and couldn't possibly have gone along with any of the violence, only to be left to die on the station.

"That's why the truth needs to be told!" He growled as he stood up to face the man.

"Whose truth?"

John had to force his voice to be calm, "The truth. That there are people who believe that by working with the Shezlan, they will have some sort of *Utopia* away from Earth. That people lost their way and decided violence was an answer, even against their own people."

"Do you know why this all started?"

John blinked but shook his head, "No."

"They are fighting against, what they believe, is a corrupt government on Tronis. They want independence from Earth. They want the government, currently in power, to be ousted and replaced with people who aren't greedy. Who aren't getting rich off the people who work to keep the system operating."

"That–that isn't happening here."

"Oh, but it is. They aren't wrong on some of their points. The Director for instance, has much invested in the orbital mining companies, as well as several companies who develop and expand the cities. He takes time with lobbyists and heeds many of their requests."

"That just supports my assessment."

"They will simply take the idea of the Shezlan being involved as some trick by the government, either the colony or Earth. They will use it as a rally cry against the corruption and further widen the gap amid the people."

"You prefer them to hate Earth rather than know the truth?"

"No, but given the other option, this is the best way to keep things stable. Presume they did believe the idea, everyone would be calling for war. Do you think we are in a state to go to war with the Prides of Thyla again?"

John had no answer. He couldn't even begin to understand the current state of Earth's military. He sat back down and rubbed his face and head. It was becoming far more complicated than getting a good story about why people served and bringing people together. It was becoming a story about conflicting conspiracies that seemed to ignore the truth.

"You ruminate on this for now, Mister Aerovant. I'll be reviewing your footage, and you'll receive what can be shared. I want you to ponder what you report."

As the door closed behind the Colonel, John felt the urge to scream. He settled for throwing his pillow at the door in defiance. It was childish, but he felt better. The Colonel infuriated him, and to make it worse, he was probably right. No one wanted to believe the truth about what had happened.

The idea that anyone would see the footage he took as proof of conspiracy, angered him. Almost as much as the fact he found what Shiekh said viable. Though he would never admit it and adamantly stamped the thought down. As much as he hated things kept secret, the people whose very job it was to tell the truth, would just twist it.

"It'll be different on Earth," he told himself.

John felt angry, he didn't believe it. He wanted to and was sure that many of his coworkers and producers would be the ones wanting the truth to come out. There was also that seed of doubt and damn that man for planting it.

"He's good at his job I guess."

There was another knock at the door. He looked at it, expecting the Colonel to return and finish the act of destroying his faith in humanity. It surprised him when it didn't open immediately. Then, there was a second knock on the door.

John got up, walked over to slide it open, and instead of seeing the Colonel, it was Silverling. She was out of her armor and black under suit; just wearing shorts and a midriff t-shirt. She looked like she had just finished a shower and held up a container of ointment.

"Could do with some help," she said with a smirk.

"I...Um..." John tripped over his own words.

Silverling smiled, "You are supposed to say, 'yes ma'am', dummy."

John chuckled, "Okay, let me try again. Hi Jakie, please come in."

"It's a start," she laughed softly.

John stepped back and motioned into the tiny space. She brushed past him, and somehow, barely touched him. It amazed him how easily she could move through a tiny space. She turned in the middle of the room and appeared to be appraising it.

"Stick you in fancy digs, don't they?"

"Well, you know, it's the whole military experience. No paint, barely comfortable, and you can access everything from your bed, slash couch, slash den."

She set the ointment down on the small counter that served as a table, and everything else. She turned back to face him and smiled crookedly. He took that moment to fully look at her and noticed she was barefoot as well.

John slid the door shut and moved over to stand by her, not sure exactly what to expect. They had only been out a few times to have some drinks and dinner. Having her in his own room never crossed his mind as possible; not just yet.

She put her arms over his shoulders and looked up at him, then moved up to kiss him. John happily accepted it, but was careful about how she meant it. The kiss was soft, not urgent, not needy, just gentle.

"I have to admit," she said, "my back still kind of hurts, so you'll have to accept the fact you're going to be reapplying it for real."

"I can do that."

"You'll also have to be on the bottom."

"Do I have a choice?"

"Not really. If you want more than a kiss."

www.ingramcontent.com/pod-product-compliance
Lightning Source LLC
Chambersburg PA
CBHW021359150726
47989CB00005B/2323